LIES

ESPECIALLY FOR GIRLS™
presents

LIES

Nancy J. Hopper

Lodestar Books
E. P. Dutton   New York

No character in this book is intended to represent any actual person;
all the incidents of the story are entirely fictional in nature.
Copyright © 1984 by Nancy J. Hopper

Library of Congress Cataloging in Publication Data

Hopper, Nancy J.
  Lies.
  "Lodestar books."
  Summary: Allison, having fallen in love with Jerry
in geometry class, is determined to go to the prom with
him, but it seems he only wants to be friends.
  [1. High schools—Fiction. 2. Schools—Fiction]
I. Title.
PZ7.H7792Li 1984 [Fic] 83-20751
ISBN 0-525-67148-X

Published in the United States by E. P. Dutton, Inc.,
2 Park Avenue, New York, N.Y. 10016

Editor: Virginia Buckley   Designer: Suzanne Haldane

Printed in the U.S.A.

to my sister, Sandra

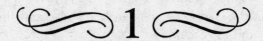

The day I fell in love was the day my problems began. As a matter of fact, I might even say falling in love was the cause of my problems, but that wouldn't exactly be true. The truth is that like most disagreeable things in my life, my latest problems seemed to sneak up on me, gradually approaching without my being aware of them, until suddenly, late in April, I was surrounded by trouble, as helpless as a tiny spider who by some bizarre accident has found itself trapped in its own web. And like the spider, I built my web myself; that is for sure.

In many ways that sleety Monday the last week in March was like any other day. I went to school, came home, raided the refrigerator, and retreated to my bedroom with my best friend, Celia Myers. Safe in my room, I put my record of

"Long-Legged Girl" on the stereo, turned it up full volume, and sat on my bed, propping one of my pillows against the headboard and making myself comfortable.

Celia sat on the yellow carpet across the room from me, next to my desk. She leaned her back against the wall behind her, her legs thrust before her, and took a drink of milk from the glass she held. She put the glass down, rested her head against the wall, and stared sightlessly straight ahead.

We had followed this routine practically every afternoon this past year, listening to my records of Elevator, thinking about school, daydreaming for a while before I turned the volume down on the stereo and we talked until Celia had to go home. About the only difference we ever made in our routine was that sometimes, usually the days Celia had to put dinner in the oven, we went to her house and listened to Elevator and daydreamed.

My room was bright, almost sunny from light through the white curtains and the reflections from the yellow carpet. If it hadn't been for the sleet on the windows and the cozy warmth of a room shut away from the outside cold, it could have been spring. I smiled to myself. I could have been a princess sitting there on my bed with its high white canopy, its fall of crisp white ruffles to the floor. Celia could have been my maid.

I subdued a laugh in my throat. Celia didn't look like a maid, sitting there, her dark blue eyes unfocused, a smear of milk at one corner of her mouth. I narrowed my eyes at her, pretending that I didn't know her, that we were strangers. How did she look, this girl?

A little strange, I decided. Celia had gathered her long, black, softly curling hair into a ponytail that morning. Being Celia, she didn't have the ponytail at the back of her head, but erupting straight from the left side. By this late in the afternoon, some hair had come loose and trailed down around her neck; the rest still stuck out like some strange growth, undecided as to its location. On anyone else, the hairstyle would have been ridiculous. On Celia, with her red, lacy, high-necked blouse, it looked only a little ridiculous, almost right.

Celia sighed. Her pink tongue stole out and licked at the smear of milk. Her eyes threatened to come into focus.

I quickly glanced away, staring at the papers scattered across the top of my desk. I didn't want to talk to Celia, not yet. I wanted to sit there and pretend I was incredibly beautiful and that Jerry Hamilton was falling in love with me.

I relaxed against the pillow and let my thoughts slide away, away from my room and Celia and the music, back to that morning in plane geometry.

Mr. Garner was late as usual. Mr. Garner's being late was the best part of plane geometry, or had been until late in January. Late January was when Jerry Hamilton moved to town and was assigned the desk next to mine.

Jerry had everything going for him. He was tall, with a narrow, dark-complexioned face, and he had the smoothest, most velvety gray eyes I had ever seen. All this was topped by thick black hair. He also had the warmest smile in the whole high school. Girls were instantly wild about him, but Jerry didn't seem the least aware of it.

Except for one rather weird exchange student from Germany, who sat directly in front of him, Jerry and I were the only juniors in a class full of sophomores. He became friends with the exchange student, Hans Spengler, almost immediately. Hans was happy to include me in their conversations, and soon Jerry was calling me his buddy. I didn't mind, not at first anyway.

That Monday both Mr. Garner and Hans were late. That

was all right by me. I hadn't finished my homework. Flipping my book open to the assignment, I grabbed the page of theorems I had been working on. It slipped from my fingers to the floor.

I leaned over to pick up the paper, reaching at the same time that Jerry did. Our fingers touched.

At that moment it happened. The fingers of his right hand brushed mine ever so lightly, but I felt the sensation of that touch the whole way up my arm, straight to my heart. I sat up in my seat, staring at Jerry.

His gray eyes met mine. The sensation spread, filling my entire body with a warm glow. My chest became tight and for a second I was unable to breathe. I was dizzy and my mouth was dry, my hands suddenly moist.

It felt a lot like the time I fell off the garage roof.

"Your paper," said Jerry, holding it out, his easy smile spreading across his narrow face.

I took it, hardly aware of the movement, my eyes fixed on his.

"Thank you," I managed. My heart resumed beating, thumping uncomfortably in my chest.

"Anything for my best buddy," said Jerry.

Buddy—somehow that seemed so distant, so cool.

Jerry went back to looking at his plane geometry book while I sat numbly holding the paper he had handed me. When Mr. Garner came into the room, I stared at him and listened to his explanations without hearing. I didn't hand in my homework sheet; I kept it to pin to my bulletin board as a souvenir of the first day, the first minute, I fell in love.

I don't remember much of the rest of my classes for that day, except for American literature, where Jerry sat behind me, and even that is mostly a blur in my mind. It seemed as if I went straight in time from sitting in geometry to sitting in my bedroom after school with Celia.

4

I was aware of a movement in the room, which was silent except for the rattle of sleet against the windows. Celia crossed the room in easy strides, lifted the arm of the stereo and settled it at the beginning of "Long-Legged Girl." That is my favorite song; hers is "Free for the Asking." She sank onto the carpet next to the machine, staring at it as if somehow the guys from Elevator would materialize from out of the record.

I wasn't ready to give up dreaming of Jerry. I let my eyes glaze over. It was a dark, romantic night, the stars twinkling, the moon a silver sliver against the black sky. Jerry held my hands and stared into my eyes. Then his head moved closer, his lips . . .

There was a knocking on the bedroom door, off beat with the music. I glanced at Celia. She twisted on the rug to look at me.

The knocking was repeated, louder. The door trembled and Celia moved to stand up.

I shook my head, my mouth forming "Mandy." Mandy is my little sister, five years old. She is a super kid, but there are times when I would like to exterminate her. She is one of the reasons I am glad my bedroom door has a lock on it. I only wish it were the kind with a key, so I could lock it while I am at school.

Mandy wouldn't give up. She pounded some more. I closed my eyes, trying to bring Jerry's lips back close to mine. There were some muffled shrieks from behind the door and the knob rattled.

Rage tore through me. I jumped from the bed and ran to the door, unlocking it, twisting the knob, and throwing it wide.

"Whatta ya want?" I screamed.

My mother jumped. All five feet, one hundred and fifty-two pounds of her left the floor for a barely discernible instant. I peered around her. Mandy was nowhere in sight.

"Mom," I said weakly.

Mother regained her composure. Behind us, Celia twisted the volume knob on the stereo. "Long-Legged Girl" faded away.

Mother was recovering fast. Her mouth closed and she took a deep steadying breath. Most people would be mad I yelled, but she wasn't. My mother's patience is endless.

"Your father called," she said in her soft Southern drawl, looking at Celia. "He said you are to be home by six." She almost said "you-all," but twenty-two years away from Tennessee had blurred the *all* into nonexistence.

"Okay," said Celia. "Thank you." She likes my mother. Most people like my mother.

Mom's eyes traveled around the room, noted the unmade bed, the papers on the desk, the books on the sunny yellow carpet, and came back to me.

"Have you girls seen Mandy?"

"No. I'm sorry I yelled at you," I said.

She didn't answer that. Instead she looked worried. "She has a cold and I told her to stay inside," she said. "I'll bet she sneaked out to the tree house."

"Do you want me to go look?"

"No, thanks. If I don't find her there, I might call for help," she said, turning away.

I closed the door gently.

"If you-all need hep, I'll hep too," said Celia in a thick Southern accent, then giggled.

"Miss Tennessee," I said, and laughed. It was a joke between us, pretending that my mother had once been Miss Tennessee.

I watched Celia change the record on the turntable to "Free for the Asking" and went back to thinking about Jerry. Maybe he was attracted to me. Maybe he liked girls of the

6

colorless, no-personality type, with pointy chins. Maybe he had touched my hand on purpose. I would never wash it again. I stared at it in awe.

"What is the matter with you?" demanded Celia. She had left the volume on low. She was ready to talk.

"Nothing," I hedged.

"Come on, Allison. You have your anemic look."

I cast her an irritated glance. Celia knows I hate being so fair skinned. She always says I look anemic when I'm depressed.

"What are you thinking about?" she probed.

"Jerry Hamilton," I admitted.

"That new kid? The one who runs around with Hans Spengler?"

I nodded. "I'm in love," I said simply.

"How do you know?"

"I know." We stared at each other. We had had crushes before, but this was the first time either of us had experienced love. I wondered if there was heartbreak ahead.

"Does he know you're alive?"

"Celia!" How could she be so cruel!

"Just asking." She grinned.

"He says we're best buddies," I told her, and my heart seemed to shrivel. I didn't want to be best buddies with Jerry. I wanted to be his steady girlfriend.

"We'll have to fix that." Her eyes flicked over my brown hair, my pointy chin, my white blouse and jeans. "Don't you have anything different to wear, something a little more—uh —feminine?"

"I have that peekaboo blouse I bought last fall."

"I know you. You'd never wear it in public."

"So I made a mistake." I shrugged. "It seemed like me in the store."

"Maybe you could borrow something of mine."

7

I didn't even answer that. Although Celia is not exactly flat-chested, the only way I could wear one of her blouses would be to leave it unbuttoned. The top half of me takes after my mom; my bottom half is skinny like my dad. That is one of the reasons I had decided the peekaboo blouse was a mistake.

"You should have picked somebody easier to fall in love with, someone who doesn't have a lot of girls after him," said Celia. She moved restlessly to my bulletin board. She didn't seem to notice the geometry paper I'd pinned there. Instead she flipped the pages of my calendar. "Another thing," she said. "He runs around with Hans Spengler. How could you possibly be serious about anyone who runs around with Hans?"

"Hans is okay," I said. When he first came from Germany last fall, Hans was all right. He was quiet and very polite and well dressed. Now he goes around cracking dumb jokes and laughing when nobody else does. He is loud and wears T-shirts with pictures of monsters on them. I think when Hans goes home in June his parents are going to be appalled at the changes in him.

Celia was frowning at the calendar. "The prom is the beginning of May. That gives us six weeks, actually only four, because no girl in her right mind would accept a date less than two weeks before the dance." She turned to look at me, her blue eyes magnetic.

"You will not believe this, Allison," she said, "but on May fifth we are going to that dance with our dream men, you with Jerry and me with a fantastic senior."

She was right. I didn't believe it. I already had a picture of the two of us, sitting in Celia's living room, watching cable television and stuffing ourselves with soft drinks and candy and chips. Sitting home with Celia the night of the prom

8

couldn't possibly be worse than my date to the Homecoming Dance with George Reese.

"Sure, Celia," I said out loud.

"You don't believe me."

"Of course I do."

That was a lie, and it seemed so innocent, so harmless, so almost true. But it was the first small strand of the web I began to build to trap myself, a web of lies to Jerry, to Mom, even to my little sister Mandy. In two short months I caused myself so much trouble that it was enough to make me swear off lying for the rest of my life.

But on that sleety day in March, I only knew I was in love. That was when my problems began.

 2

The fact of the matter is that there are people who are addicted to drink and people who are addicted to drugs. Then there is me, Allison Anne Witmer, who is addicted to lying. For years I pretended it was a sort of hobby of mine, an inconvenient one that caused trouble at times, but one that was worth the risks. Besides, like the dark brown color of my eyes and of my hair, the fact that elaborate untrue statements came out of my mouth was a big part of me for as long as I could remember. It has always been a personality trait that I could never really change no matter how hard I have tried —and believe me, I have tried.

And I never really caused a major castrophe with my lying until I fell in love with Jerry. Then I found out exactly what this very dangerous hobby could cost me.

"Be alluring and desirable," Celia had instructed me. "But most of all, be mysterious. That is the most important part. Men love mysterious women. They look on them as a challenge."

That was all right for Celia to say. She was way ahead of me in the mysterious department. That is partly a result of her slightly tilted eyes, but mostly because her parents are divorced. I know a lot of kids whose parents are divorced, but Celia is the only girl I know whose parents are divorced with her living with her father. That might not sound very mysterious to a lot of people, but compared with me, whose parents are not only still married but living together, it is very mysterious.

Nevertheless, I promised to do my best. I got up early the next morning and spent an entire hour working on my appearance. I smoothed by best feature—shiny brown shoulder-length hair—back from my face in a sophisticated style, wore my biggest hoop earrings, and made up my face to accent my brown eyes. I used blush to minimize my broad forehead, but I figured there wasn't a thing I could do about my pointy chin, so I ignored it. Then I put on my blue blouse with the puffy sleeves and wrapped a wide orange sash around my waist to emphasize my figure. Feeling very daring, not at all like me, I went off to school.

"Not bad," admitted Celia when we met at our lockers. She ran her eyes down over me. "You have a terrific figure." Then she frowned. "But did you have to wear sneakers?"

"I always wear sneakers with jeans, even in winter. It's sort of a trademark with me."

"They don't go with the eye shadow and hoop earrings. You should have worn high-heeled sandals, something to make your feet look more attractive."

Somehow I couldn't imagine anything that could possibly

make my feet look more attractive, but I didn't say so. Instead, I asked, "What's that awful smell?"

"I don't smell anything."

"Like someone spilled a bottle of perfume."

Celia narrowed her eyes at me. "It's Eau d'Intrigue," she said. "I'm trying to attract a certain boy's attention in French."

"Where's he sit, the other side of the room?"

At that moment the warning bell rang, and we hurried off to our separate first-period classes.

Somehow I lasted through the first two periods of the day, until it was time for geometry. I hurried to the room and peered into the door. Jerry was in his seat next to mine. Hans was there too, in front of Jerry. Hans was pretending to be the greatest rock drummer of all time. He had his head bent and his eyes closed and was drumming with his two index fingers on his desk top.

I took a deep breath and let it out slowly. Then I relaxed my shoulders, my neck, my spine. I sauntered casually into the room, my hips swaying slightly, my walk languid and graceful. I passed Hans and stopped between Jerry's and my desks.

Jerry was puzzling over his homework.

"Hello, Jerry," I said in a throaty voice.

"Hunh?" He looked up, his eye bewildered.

"I said, 'Hello,' " I repeated, lowering my eyelashes and then very slowly lifting them again.

"Oh, hi," he muttered, his eyes back on his paper.

"Duh, duh," said Hans, drumming away. "Da, da, dah!"

I sat, crossing my legs gracefully, lowering my lashes part-way and staring boldly at Jerry. He didn't notice either my bold looks or my blue blouse and the orange sash. I don't think he would have noticed if I had been wearing army fatigues unbuttoned to the waist.

It seemed to take forever, but at last he glanced up. Our eyes met.

"Did you figure out number three?" he asked.

I hesitated, considering, then slowly licked my lips.

Behind Jerry, Frances Wilson stared intently at me. She always stares intently; that's what she's best at. She hardly ever speaks, even when someone speaks to her.

I ignored her, concentrating on Jerry, trying to think of a witty answer to number three. There aren't many witty answers in plane geometry.

In front of Jerry, Hans made a sudden darting movement with his right hand toward an imaginary cymbal. He gave one last loud, "Duh, dah!" and spun in his seat, throwing his arms wide.

"Hi, group," he yelled, loud enough to be heard outside. "What's happening?"

"I was wondering—" said Jerry, seeming to forget all about the third theorem and ignoring Hans.

"Hi, gorgeous," shouted Hans, even louder.

"Hi, Hans." I could have killed him.

"Where's your beautiful friend?"

"What beautiful friend?" At that point the only beautiful friend I could think of was Jerry.

"Sweet Celia." He wiggled his eyebrows suggestively and smacked his lips. It is amazing how a basically attractive boy like Hans can make himself look so repulsive.

"She has gym this period," I said coldly, "like every Tuesday this period."

I glanced at Jerry. He was looking at Hans with a sort of angry stare. My heart lurched. Maybe Jerry was going to ask me out and Hans had interrupted! I wet my lips and was preparing another smile when Mr. Garner rushed into the room and started talking to us about the proofs we had to learn to do if we wanted to pass the course.

I didn't learn much that period. I don't think Jerry did either. Every time I sneaked a glance at him, he was staring off into space. I was tempted to think he was daydreaming about our romance, but if he had been, he at least would have looked in my direction now and then.

Jerry didn't seem to notice Hans, which was amazing in itself. Hans spent the entire class humming rock tunes in varying degrees of loudness. He also answered more of Mr. Garner's questions than anyone else. I think one of Hans' problems is that he seems to have studied everything we have in school before he came to this country. Therefore he is bored out of his mind sitting in our classes and tries to amuse himself in other ways. Sometimes those ways can be pretty spectacular.

When the bell rang, I took my time gathering my books together. Jerry's next class is on the opposite side of the building from mine, so we don't go the same direction. I wanted to give him a good chance to tell me what he had been wondering about.

He almost forgot. With a sort of staring expression on his face, he got his books together and wandered toward the classroom door.

"Jerry!" I hurried to catch him.

"What?" He sounded a little annoyed.

"You were going to ask me something."

"I was?"

"Yes." I could feel my cheeks burning. "You said you were wondering about something, and then Hans interrupted to ask about Celia." Hans is always asking me about Celia.

"Oh, yes." His eyes lit up.

"Well—" I wondered if I was more attractive, more desirable, with flaming cheeks.

"Do you know Stephanie Harris?"

Stephanie Harris! Of course I know Stephanie Harris. Everybody knows Stephanie. She is tall and willowy and graceful. She has very unusual hair, a sort of reddish gold that tumbles to her shoulders in a mass of curls. She has a clear, creamy complexion and greenish blue eyes and fine bone structure. She also has a terrific personality. I think I hate her.

"Yes," I admitted. I swallowed, my throat tight.

Jerry looked a little shy. "I wonder if you could find something out for me."

"Sure." My throat closed. I was practically choking. Maybe I had some strange disease and would die in the next half hour. Maybe I would die, right now, at Jerry's feet, and he wouldn't even notice.

"Can you find out if she's going with anyone?"

Aaargh!

I didn't answer. I couldn't.

"Will you?" asked Jerry, his gray eyes desperate.

"Sure, yes. Okay," I muttered.

"Thanks." He smiled, suddenly happy. "I knew you would." He punched me lightly on my right shoulder. "You're a real great buddy."

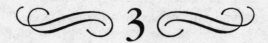

3

A real great buddy. Just what I'd always dreamed of our relationship, buddies. I was doomed to go through the years listening to Jerry's love life with other girls, helping him to make contact with potential girlfriends while I sat at home and suffered from unrequited love.

I found out about Stephanie for him. I found out all about her. For instance, I found out that her reddish gold curls were perfectly natural and that she was an honor-roll student as well as a member of the dramatic club and a saxophone player in the band. I also discovered, much to my misery, that she was currently between boyfriends.

Of course I didn't tell Jerry all that. I only told him that I was working on it. As a reward I received another punch on the shoulder and the words of "Thanks, kid!"

By the time Friday after school rolled around, I was actually glad for the weekend, when I didn't have to see Jerry's face for two whole days. I was relieved that Celia had taken up belly dancing to improve her "posture and posterior" and that this was her very first lesson and I didn't have to listen to her stale old words of sympathy. I was only too happy to slink off to my room and suffer my wounds in private.

My mood was not improved when I arrived home to the sound of my mother and father arguing. My dad is a dentist; he tries to take most Fridays off so that he has a three-day weekend to recover from what he calls the pressures of dental decision making. From the sounds of things, he should have stayed at work. It would have been cheerier filling cavities.

At least they were in the kitchen and neither of them noticed me. I didn't have to pretend false joy. I hesitated, listening for a couple of minutes, sort of testing the air to find out what the weekend would be like.

It was not promising.

I went to my bedroom and closed the door, safe in my own sanctuary where I could suffer over my doomed love alone. I turned from the door to see my kid sister poking around in the stuff on my dresser.

I looked at her, trying to decide whether to yell or to play the part of the huge-hearted older sister. It was a delicate decision. I didn't want Mandy to get the idea she could nose around in my room, but at the moment she seemed to be the only person in the entire house who was happy, and I hated to spread despair. All this went through my mind while I assessed the situation.

She was into my lipstick, fortunately not my best lipstick. She had smeared dark red over her lips and halfway across one cheek. While I watched her, she gave a big nervous grin.

17

The lipstick was smeared in red gobs across the tips of her little white baby teeth. She looked like a very young vampire.

Taking firm control of myself, I pushed down the urge to shout at her. Instead, I carefully made my voice sound very low and sad, no trick at all that day. "Didn't Mother ever tell you you have to be thirteen before you wear lipstick?" I asked.

"No." She relaxed a little.

"Tsk, tsk." I shook my head. "She must be slipping."

Mandy rolled her pale blue eyes at the mirror and then back at me.

"Don't you know that lipstick is made of shark fat?" I said. "And if you put shark fat on your lips before you are thirteen, you will turn into a shark?"

"No." She sounded a little uncertain.

"For sure." I smiled pleasantly. "Where do you think sharks come from anyway? They are children who have tasted lipstick before they are thirteen."

Mandy gave a little giggle, but she looked worried.

"Ah, well," I said, turning my back on her and reassembling the tubes and bottles on my dresser top. "Dad will have to drive you down to the beach and throw you into the lake Sunday. It's too bad you haven't learned to swim yet."

"Mom!" Mandy ran out of my room. "Mommy!"

I threw myself on my bed and laughed until the tears came. Then I cried a little, mourning that my own true love was in love with Stephanie Harris.

Finally I sat up and wiped the tears from my eyes, hiccuping gently. I went to look at my bulletin board. It wasn't as large as Celia's, and the things on it were a lot different from what Celia had on hers. For instance, there were three large photographs from last year when I was into photography. My brother Ron and I were in the same class and went out together taking pictures. My favorite was one taken at the old pottery of a bunch of weeds going to seed against a weathered brick wall. I touched it gently with one finger, thinking of that bright afternoon and of Ron and how much I missed him now that he was in college. Maybe he could have helped me with my problems. I felt a sharp stab of loneliness, like homesickness, for him.

I pushed the feeling to one side and began rearranging the bulletin board. I left the pictures where they were, but took down a list of New Year's resolutions and a withered corsage of gardenias from the Homecoming Dance. I threw those and some programs from plays and an old basketball schedule away, then tacked up the latest school newspaper and a program from a community concert I had gone to with Mom. I gave the geometry paper a place of honor. When I finished, there was a lot of empty space. I stared at the space and wondered if Ron would like to go taking pictures again this summer; or maybe I could go without him. I had signed up for advanced photography next fall at school, and it would be good to get some practice.

I wandered over to my desk and started shifting things around on it. I took my antique Shirley Temple doll that Aunt Joy had given me and moved it to my dresser, then put my magazines and books into two separate piles. Finally I sat down and took a piece of paper from the center drawer. I sat and stared at it while I dreamed of ways of making myself so irresistible that Jerry wouldn't think of me as a buddy anymore.

I felt as if I were being watched. I shook my head and concentrated on the paper, trying to ease back into my dreams. I still felt that way. I turned toward my doorway.

Mandy was peering around the frame, one pale blue eye and the top of frizzy blond hair exposed. The smear of lipstick across her cheek had been removed, leaving a pink stain which resembled a birthmark.

"What do you want?" I demanded.

Mandy came out from behind the frame and entered my room. She had both arms behind her back and she looked a little guilty.

"Mom said I was to stay out of your things," she said. "She said I wasn't to bother you, that you had important things on your mind."

I nodded. Mom had no idea how important.

"She said to tell you I'm sorry."

"Are you?"

Mandy frowned. "No," she said.

I almost laughed.

"I like to get into your things," she added.

"If you do, we'll just have to send you back where you came from," I told her.

"You can't. I grew in Mom's body and I'm too big now," she said.

"Where did you find that out?" None of Mom's friends was pregnant.

"Mom told me. Besides, Mrs. Johnston told us in kindergarten. She showed us a film of a baby cow being born. Also, we have a tank of guppies in our room, and they are always making more."

Things sure were different when I was in kindergarten. All they taught us about reproduction had to do with growing marigolds from seeds.

"I meant send you back where you really came from," I said, keeping my face expressionless.

"Where's that?" She looked suspicious.

"If I tell you, you'll just go running to Mom." I glanced back at my desk.

"No, I won't." She came a step closer. "Tell me, Allison, Please."

"Naw. You can't keep a secret."

"I can." She wiggled with excitement.

"You came from the planet of the apes."

"That's a movie. I saw it on television."

"It was based on true facts. Two apes dropped you off here on the way to Hollywood to make the movie."

"You're teasing me." Mandy smiled as if she liked being teased.

"Am not," I said seriously. "Mom and Dad named you after the miniature poodle that we had."

"A dog?"

"It died."

Mandy considered this. She came closer, leaning on my desk with one arm. The other arm was still behind her back.

"Were you sad when the dog died?" she asked.

"Yes," I said. "I cried." We really did have a poodle and it really did die. I hadn't thought about that dog in a long time.

"I'd like to have a little puppy, but Mom said I should get a goldfish," said Mandy. She sounded very disgusted.

I couldn't blame her. A goldfish was a long way from a dog. I resolved to put the pressure on Mom for a puppy. Maybe I could offer to take care of it.

"I brought you something," said Mandy, finally bringing her other arm out from behind her back. "Here."

It was a photocopy of what looked like a page from a coloring book. It was a picture of a sort of chunky-looking man standing behind a tree and holding a bag of candy. There was a pretty little girl walking down the sidewalk, and he was smiling at her. *Don't Talk to Strangers* was the caption under the picture. Mandy had colored it, staying within the lines in most places.

"I colored it at school," she said.

"Thanks." I studied the picture. It wasn't my idea of an attractive wall decoration, but I could hardly hurt her feelings by tossing it in the wastebasket. I heaved myself up from my desk chair and pinned the thing to a bare spot on my bulletin board.

I looked back at my desk. Where was I? Oh, yes, thinking about Jerry. I glanced at Mandy. She was staring at me, giving me adoring looks. I can't understand it. I tell her lies and am mean to her and tell her to get lost and to stay out of my room, and she still thinks I am the greatest invention since pizza.

I took a deep breath. My immediate problem was to get her out of my room without a battle. Then I could go back to daydreaming about Jerry.

"I'll give you a present if you promise not to bother me," I said.

"Okay!"

"Here." I handed her the lipstick she had ruined. I prefer lip gloss anyway.

"Thanks!" Her eyes went big. She grabbed the lipstick and dashed out of my room before I could change my mind.

"Hey!" I yelled after her.

"What?" She was already down the hall by the top of the stairs.

"Don't use it until you're thirteen. You might turn into a shark."

4

Mandy used the lipstick I had given her to draw round spots like a clown's on her cheeks. Then she drew round red spots on every doll she owned and even on her teddy bear. She was busily drawing red spots on the bathroom mirror when Mom caught up with her. Somehow Mom seemed to consider this my fault.

By the time Celia called Saturday morning and invited me to lunch, I was glad for any excuse to get out of the house. Mom and Dad were still not on the best of terms. Mom's usual smile was missing and even her Southern accent sounded curt. Dad announced that he was going to the office to check supplies. I had always thought his office help did that, but I didn't say so. I know when to keep a low profile.

"Wait till you see what I learned yesterday!" said Celia

when she answered the door. "That class is absolutely great, terrific."

I followed her into the kitchen and helped her serve lunch. The whole way through lunch and through washing the dishes, she chattered about belly dancing, her fantastic teacher, and the other students. I muttered an occasional grunt. By the time we went to her room, I was thinking I should have offered to help my dad check supplies.

Celia went to her stereo and put on a record. I was expecting an Elevator record. She has the largest collection of anyone I know and a big collection of Journey too. The speakers made a little snickering sound and then the music came on. It had a strange Middle Eastern twanging sound.

Celia struck a pose in the middle of her bedroom, one arm over her head, the other at her side, hand on hip. Her right hip jutted sharply to one side; her butt stuck out in the rear. She lowered her head, then raised it dramatically, a solemn expression on her face.

I bit my lower lip, trying not to laugh. When I couldn't hold it any longer, I covered it with a series of coughs.

Celia didn't seem to notice. The music became frenzied. She moved her pelvis in a series of forward and sidewise jerks. Then she stood with her feet motionless and slowly rotated her pelvis.

I could feel my eyes widen. My laughter died in my throat. Celia took a couple of steps forward and repeated the pelvic motions. Then she lowered her arms and shut off the stereo.

"That's what we learned yesterday," she said, smiling at me.

"That's obscene!" I burst out.

"What do you mean, obscene? Belly dancing is an ancient art."

"But Celia, those motions. They look exactly like—"

"I told you it's an art!" she yelled at me. She glared. "You'll see. Wait till our recital."

"You mean you'd do that in *public?*"

"I guess I can't expect you to understand," she said loftily.

I sighed, then burped. I felt as if I was getting indigestion. Celia had made us a chicken curry for lunch and served it with green grapes. Maybe it went with the belly dancing. It sure didn't go with the cold pizza I had eaten for breakfast.

"I wonder why they always hold the prom in May," I said, trying to get onto a safe subject.

"Probably because of some pagan rite that's been continued through the ages," said Celia, looking through her records. "Colleges used to hold a big dance on May first and elect a queen and have a group of girls dance around a maypole." She hesitated, putting down the records. "My mother was May queen when she was a senior in college. My dad says it gave her such a big head that she never recovered, and that's why she ran away and left him and me to face life alone."

That was a new one to me: Celia's mother had been a May queen. Celia doesn't mention her mother very often. When she does, it's never anything complimentary. I had always thought of the woman as having a face like a day-old baked apple and the personality of a professional hockey player.

Celia was looking a little pinched, as if she had revealed too much. I hurried to act as if I'd barely heard it.

"In Russia on May Day they hold a parade," I said. "If we lived there, we would get to march in groups holding flowers and to look at all the tanks and armored vehicles."

"And handsome cossacks."

"I didn't know cossacks were handsome," I said. "I thought they were coarse and smelly and violent."

"Strong men," said Celia dreamily. "Tough, with good teeth."

Either Celia was into this exotic Eastern thing more than I suspected or she had been watching too much cable TV. That, or else . . .

"You have any particular strong man in mind?" I asked casually.

"Lee Favazzo," said Celia, a faraway look in her blue eyes.

"Lee Favazzo!"

"Something wrong with that?"

"No. It's only that—" How could I finish? I mean, Lee Favazzo.

"That he is tall and has black hair and eyes and the sexiest smile and a fantastic build," said Celia.

"Right."

"And that he's president of the senior class and the honor society and lettered in two sports."

"Right."

"And has been going steady with Missy Kessler for two years."

"You got it."

"Little problems." She shrugged.

Poor Celia. She had gone completely round the bend.

I leaned forward, resting an elbow on a knee and my chin in the palm of one hand. Sitting this way is a habit I am trying to encourage. Celia says I have a beautiful heart-shaped face, but I know I have a broad forehead like a Mongolian tribesman and a very pointy chin.

"Besides," continued Celia, a crafty look replacing the dazed expression in her eyes. "I heard that he and Missy are going to break up."

"Sure," I said gloomily. "That doesn't mean he'll date you." Facing the prom with Jerry dating Stephanie was bad enough. Facing it with a best friend out of her gourd over Mr. Unobtainable was going to be the pits.

"How 'bout you, Allison?" she asked, her voice going hard, stung because I didn't fall in with her fantasy over Lee. "How are you getting along with Jerry?"

"Not great," I admitted.

"Oh well. He's only a junior anyway."

"So what?"

"Practically a child. I like older men."

I glared at her. "He might not be the super Lee Favazzo—" I began.

"Besides, I thought you said you and Jerry are buddies," she cut in.

I groaned inwardly.

"Isn't he always asking your advice about girls?" she pushed. "He's more like a friend, a brother—"

"Will you shut up!"

There was a few minutes' silence. I looked at Celia's walls. A person could trace Celia's life by studying those walls. There was a series of pictures of her as a child in a ballerina costume, and a smallish picture of Spiderman. There was a big picture of Matt Dillon, and there was a color photograph of Prince Charles and Lady Diana from a time when Celia was a little nutty over an English exchange student. I stood up and crossed to her bulletin board, which also had pictures on it. There was one of Lee Favazzo, obviously cut out of last year's yearbook. It was surrounded by valentine hearts. I closed my eyes.

Celia was talking to me, her voice softer, saying something about how we had five weeks to the dance and that we could still get dates with Lee and Jerry and then our lives would be wonderful.

"After all," she finished, "if we really want something bad enough, we should be able to get it."

"For years I wanted Amanda to be adopted by someone

27

in California," I pointed out, "but it never once happened."

"This is different," said Celia. "This is wanting something within reason."

Something within reason. If Celia thought there was the slightest chance of Lee Favazzo's ever asking her anywhere, she was in worse shape than I'd thought.

"I called him this morning," she confided.

"On the phone?" Even to my own ears my voice sounded surprised.

"Of course on the phone. I asked what our chemistry assignment was."

"But you don't have chemistry."

"Neither does Lee." She looked very self-satisfied. "It was a way to get his attention."

"So—"

"So what?"

"What did he say?" I wanted to grab her and shake her.

"That he would get Hans, since Hans is living with them this semester and he has chemistry."

I had a sudden vision of Hans drumming away at the dinner table and felt a surge of sympathy for the Favazzos.

"He said, 'Ah, my little turtledove.' "

"Lee?"

"No, Hans. He had just gotten home from a W. C. Fields movie with Jerry. Fields called every woman in it a little turtledove."

"What did you and Hans talk about?"

"About his chemistry class, and then we talked about the differences between German and American schools. When I got tired of hearing his hot breath in the receiver, I told him I had to hang up and go do my homework."

"What about Lee?"

"Monday I go into plan B, to make him notice me physically."

"How?"

"Maybe I'll show him my belly dance."

"You can't do that!"

"I can too."

"What if some teacher sees you? You'll get suspended from school."

"I'll tell them it's part of my religion."

I looked at her. Sometimes I can't tell when Celia is joking and when she is not. I certainly hoped that this time she was joking.

"I'd give anything to go to that dance with Lee," she said.

Personally, I wanted to go to the dance, but I didn't figure my life would be over if I didn't. "I don't care about the prom," I said recklessly. "I only care about Jerry."

"What you have to do is shock him out of his image of you," said Celia. "Make him really look at you, recognize you as a female instead of some neutral buddy-type person."

"I feel like a passionate woman captured inside the body of an ordinary teenage girl," I mourned.

"You have to experiment more until you find the right key, become the right *you* to unlock his responses."

It sounded like another form of lying.

"You have to be so absolutely fascinating that every head will turn, every breath will catch, and every heart will hesitate when you enter a room."

"You've been reading beauty magazines again."

Celia didn't seem to hear me. She was rummaging through the pots and jars and bottles on her dresser. "Want to borrow my purple eye shadow?"

"No, thanks."

"Silver? I'll need it back for Hat Day, but you can use it until then."

"I don't know. I think maybe Jerry goes more for natural good looks."

29

There was a silence while Celia considered my natural looks and said nothing.

"I decided that from making this big study of Stephanie and everything about her," I said. "It's all natural: her hair, her eyes, her complexion, figure, everything."

More silence.

"Why can't I just be me!" I burst out. "Why can't Jerry like me the way I am!"

"He does," said Celia in a hurry. "He only has to *notice* you a little more. You have to take advantage of your assets."

There, she had said it—my assets. That is one of the reasons I like Celia as a best friend. No matter how bad a situation is, she can always find something to make it seem better.

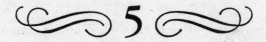

Monday I went to school with a whole new image, the whole-some look. Maybe Jerry went for the scrubbed healthy type, the girl who looks as if she just got home from jogging ten miles and drinks gallons and gallons of orange juice. I have never once jogged, and I only drink orange juice in order to prevent colds and scurvy, but since he was new at our school I didn't think Jerry could possibly know that about me.

I dug into the back of my closet and came out with a white V-neck T-shirt with cap sleeves and a pointy collar. I put on my tightest jeans and a pair of new white sneakers.

I also borrowed Mom's tennis racket, thinking that it would make a nice touch. The only problem was that it must have been quite old; it had a laminated wood frame and was kept in a press.

"You can use the racket, but don't take the press off except to play," said Mom. "I've had that racket a long time and I've always taken very good care of it."

"I'm not going to play." I examined the racket. It was a pretty good-looking piece of equipment, with its different colors of natural woods and a black leather grip. With the press it must have weighed five pounds.

"Then why do you want to borrow it?"

"I'm building up to the idea of physical exercise."

Mom gave me a look, but she didn't ask any more questions. I lugged the tennis racket and my books and my purse off to school. Naturally, the racket in the press wouldn't fit in my locker, so I had to carry it with me to classes, which didn't upset me. Otherwise, Jerry wouldn't have seen me with it.

At least the tennis racket attracted Jerry's attention. He came into geometry as I was trying to load all my stuff on my desk top and still have space to spread out a paper to work on. He approached from behind and put a hand on my shoulder.

I felt that hand through my whole body.

He shouldn't be allowed to do that, I thought to myself. He could short-circuit somebody. A vision of female bodies, all electrocuted by Jerry's touch, filled my mind. They were littered over the floors of our high school, while Jerry went merrily on his way, completely oblivious to the destruction behind him.

"I didn't know you play tennis," he said, sliding into his seat opposite mine and eyeing me with approval. "That's a great game."

"I play some," I said modestly. Actually I had played twice when I was thirteen and had given it up as a hot sweaty game.

"I don't care what anyone says about racquetball," said

Jerry. "Tennis requires much more skill and endurance."

"Oh, definitely." I didn't know a thing about racquetball either.

"Why the wood racket?" He took it from my desk, examining it more closely.

"It's my lucky racket. I've had it a long time."

"Must have. Not many kids use these." He put it carefully back on top of my desk.

"I got it when I was two," I said.

"Two!"

"Yeah. Heh. My dad's a tennis nut. He started taking me to the courts when I was a little kid." Watch it, Allison, a small sense of self-survival warned me. I ignored it.

"Maybe I'll see you there," said Jerry. "I'm going out for the boys' team. Do you practice at the same time?"

"I stopped playing in town," I improvised. "At least in the past three or four years. I go to the indoor courts in Akron. My dad takes me."

"I didn't know there was anyone that serious about tennis around here," said Jerry, his gray eyes filling with respect. "You're probably top seed on the girls' team."

"I don't play with the high school," I said airily, with a touch of the professional who doesn't want to embarrass the amateurs.

"I see," said Jerry. Then, losing interest in my physical prowess, he asked, "Did you find out about Stephanie?"

"What about her?" My tones formed ice, but he didn't notice.

"Is she going with anyone?"

"I couldn't find out."

"Oh."

"I don't know, Jerry," I said. "I don't think Stephanie is exactly the kind of girl you would like."

33

"What do you mean?"

"I think—" All of a sudden I had an inspiration. "I think she's into drugs."

"Drugs?"

"Pot, pills." I shrugged. "I'm not sure."

"Where'd you hear that?"

"Around." I hesitated, then went on. "I heard she was picked up by the police."

Jerry looked shaken. It was obvious that kids who did drugs were not Jerry's type, not his type at all.

I felt a sudden surge of joy, immediately followed by an uneasy sneaking doubt. I was making this up. It could be true, I told myself stubbornly. Yeah, sure, said another part. Stephanie could be secretly married and have two kids too.

I glanced at Fran Wilson. She was leaning forward, her eyes intent, a funny expression on her face. If she had been a dog, her ears would have been pricked up to catch every word.

"Of course it's probably only a rumor," I said hastily, but it was too late. Hans came into class, followed by Mr. Garner. Jerry slumped in his seat, watching Mr. Garner and looking very unhappy. Fran stared at me steadily, unblinking.

Allison, you rat, I told myself. You have got to tell Jerry you made that up.

But I didn't. Instead I sat through all my classes, not listening to my teachers, not even paying attention to the kids around me, thinking about that last awful lie I had told Jerry. At least once during the day I made myself a solemn promise that in last-period American literature, I would turn around in my seat, put on my most innocent look, and confess to Jerry that there was not one word of truth in that story I told him about Stephanie.

I did manage to set Fran Wilson straight. She and I ended

34

up next to each other in line at the salad bar in the cafeteria. We both reached for the Italian dressing at the same time.

"You first," I said.

She carefully lifted the ladle, poured dressing all over her salad, refilled the ladle, and poured a second time.

"I checked out that rumor," I said quietly so that no one else could hear. "The one about Stephanie."

Fran looked at me. She has pretty hazel eyes; rather, they would be pretty if they didn't always look into a person instead of at her.

"And it's only a rumor," I said, my voice going louder. "Just a rumor." I knew Fran wasn't deaf, but sometimes she sure seemed it. She held out the ladle and I took it.

"Understand?" I asked, sweating. I didn't think Fran would tell anyone else, but I had to be certain.

"Yes," she whispered.

That wasn't too awful, I told myself, ignoring the fact that I was weak from the effort. Look on it as practice on how to tell Jerry.

The rest of the day seemed endless. My brain kept churning over and over that I was a horrible monster, that I had made up ugly lies to make Stephanie seem less, and equally devious ones to make myself seem more. My only way out was to tell Jerry in literature class that every word was untrue, that basically I didn't know anything about tennis, and that Stephanie was a very nice person who didn't ever try drugs, not that I knew about anyway.

I went into American literature determined to tell Jerry the truth. I sat through the entire period trying to think up answers to the questions he was certain to ask: Where did I hear the rumor? Who told it? Did Stephanie know about it? Jerry was a lot more inquisitive than Fran.

The bell rang to dismiss class.

I didn't tell Jerry.

I just couldn't.

Instead I tried to make a bargain with fate and a promise to myself. If Jerry didn't find out about this last horrible lie I told him, I would never tell another lie in my entire life.

6

"Call him on the phone," advised Celia as soon as she'd heard of my latest disaster. "It's always easier to confess to somebody if you don't have to look him in the eyes."

"I can't," I said miserably.

"Can't never did anything," said Celia, sounding like my mother. "Besides, if you are really interested in Jerry, you should call him anyway. You have to keep in his mind all the time, not only while you are at school."

"Yeah," I said without enthusiasm. I know lots of girls who call boys. I am not one of them.

"He's going to find out sooner or later anyway," she pushed.

I curled into a ball, hugging my knees to my chest. "Candy Heart" was on the stereo. It was at the part where the heart was melting.

"Remember the time in the eighth grade when you told the whole school you had leukemia and only had a year to live?" asked Celia brightly.

I groaned. I had only told four or five people, but word got around fast.

"How all the teachers and the kids were so nice to you until they found out it wasn't true?"

"What does that have to do with now?" I asked sourly. I had enough trouble without being reminded of past blunders.

"Well, if you had confessed right in the beginning that it was a whopper, then the school wouldn't have called your parents and everybody wouldn't have been mad at you."

"And I wouldn't have sworn off lying for the rest of my life."

"I guess you had plenty of time to think about it all those weeks you were grounded," said Celia, cheerful as ever. She can talk of the most horrible tragedies in the happiest of tones.

When I didn't answer, she continued, "You can pretend to Jerry you called about Hat Day."

That wasn't a bad idea. I relaxed a little, freeing my legs. My feet had fallen asleep. I beat my heels on her shaggy rug, trying to work the pins and needles out of them. Hat Day was the following week. Every student and every teacher was supposed to wear a hat or costume signifying the person they admired most in history. I wanted to wear the hat of some fiercely attractive woman to catch Jerry's attention and make him think of me as something more than a great buddy.

"The best I can come up with is Madame Curie," I complained.

"Pick someone more romantic. Madame Curie reminds me of chemistry labs and horrible smells." For someone who wouldn't give me the slightest hint of whose hat she was wearing, Celia was terribly interested in my choice.

"Chris Evert Lloyd," I said. "She has a great figure and is tanned and wholesome looking."

"If you really think of a sweatband as being romantic—"

"Scratch Ms. Lloyd." I chewed at a fingernail, silently wondering if I should consider Celia's advice. Last year she went to school as Lizzie Borden, the axe murderess. She wore a big straw hat covered with red paint to simulate blood.

"I know," said Celia. "You can be Tokyo Rose. She was a famous spy of World War II."

"What kind of hats did she wear?"

"I don't know. You can't expect me to do all the work." Celia looked thoughtful. "I think she went around with a rose between her teeth."

Somehow I had to doubt it. I mean, if she were a famous spy and she went around with a rose in her teeth, how could she do any spying? People would recognize her.

"I'll think about it," I promised.

"And call Jerry right now. You can use the phone in my dad's room. I won't even listen."

"I can't," I said, standing and stamping my feet. All the pins and needles were gone, but they still felt a little numb. "I promised Mom I'd be home early. Today is parent-teacher conference day in the elementary school. I have to sit for Mandy."

It took me three whole days to gather up the courage to call Jerry. Meanwhile my life was a depressing mess. I could barely look at him in school and I couldn't concentrate on my classes either. Finally, Thursday after dinner I gathered up my courage. I crept upstairs and went to my parents' bedroom where there is a private extension to the telephone. I closed the door and sat on the soft blue rug and pulled the telephone down beside me. Then I took a couple of deep breaths and practiced saying "hello" several times in a warm and sexy voice.

When at last I picked up the receiver, the palms of my hands were sweating so badly that it almost slipped from my grasp. I dialed the numbers with shaking fingers and waited. The phone only rang twice.

"Hello," said a woman's voice.

I almost hung up.

"Is Jerry there?" I squeaked.

"Just a minute. Jerry. Jerry! Telephone!"

I was glad I was sitting on the floor. Otherwise I would have tumbled over in a heap. As it was, I leaned forward and braced my elbows on my knees.

"This is Allison," I said when Jerry finally came to the phone.

"Hi, Allison." He didn't sound pleased or surprised or anything.

I had notes on a piece of paper. Celia and I had worked on it together. Supposedly, casual conversation came first and then I built to telling him I lied about Stephanie and then we went back to casual conversation. It all sounded so easy if I didn't think about it.

"I wanted to ask you about our literature assignment." I said in a mechanical fashion, reading from the paper.

"We didn't have one."

"Wasn't Jill Anderson funny in geometry today?" I asked, still reading from the list.

"Er, I guess so."

"What are you wearing to Hat Day?" I blurted. Next after that I was supposed to tell him I made up that rumor about Stephanie. I crumpled the paper in one fist.

40

"I don't know yet. We didn't have Hat Day at my last school," said Jerry. "Who are you going as?"

"I'll never tell," I said in a low throaty voice, then chuckled. The chuckle turned into a nervous giggle. Now, I told myself. Now! Tell him casually that the story about Stephanie isn't true. If he asks where you heard it, say you don't remember. I inhaled deeply.

On Jerry's end of the line there were the crashing of dishes in the background and a lot of people talking. It almost sounded as if there were a party going on. On my end there was only the harsh sound of my breathing.

"I found out that Stephanie isn't going with anyone," said Jerry.

"She isn't?" I tried to sound surprised.

"No. There are about six guys interested in her though. That doesn't give me much of a chance."

"I don't know," I said. I would prefer Jerry over anybody.

"She hardly knows I'm alive. I tried to talk with her in typing and she gave me this nice smile and then sort of ducked her head over her typewriter."

"Maybe she's shy." Now, I thought to myself. Tell him you lied. At least tell him the rumor isn't true.

"You think?" He sounded hopeful. Maybe he didn't care if Stephanie was a pothead. Maybe he didn't believe what I said, or maybe he had forgotten I said it. I hoped so.

"Lots of girls are shy, even the pretty and popular ones," I said while my brain scurried around, confused by the turn the conversation had taken.

"I think it's my fault," said Jerry, falling into despair again. "When I'm around her, something seems to happen to me. I can't think of anything to say. She looks at me and I sort of freeze up."

"You could call her on the phone," I suggested. "That

might be easier. You wouldn't have to look at her when you talked."

"What could I say?"

"Ask her about Hat Day. Tell her something funny that happened in one of your classes." Suddenly I relaxed. Jerry and I were talking normally, just like at school.

"That's a great idea."

"Thanks," I said modestly.

"I don't know what I'd do without you. See you tomorrow," said Jerry and he hung up.

I sat staring at the receiver and then slowly hung up too. Only then did I realize what had happened. I hadn't confessed to Jerry that I lied and I had told him to call another girl. I had practically shoved him at Stephanie Harris. I thought I was going to throw up all over the blue rug.

I whimpered out loud. Then I drew my knees up and wrapped my arms around them, the way I used to when I was little and was upset. How could I do such a thing? How could I be so dumb? I put my head on my knees, rocking gently back and forth. Tears filled my eyes.

The door opened and Mandy walked in.

"Get out!" I screamed. "Don't you ever dare to come into my room without knocking!"

She ran.

A few seconds later the door opened a crack and she peeked in at me.

"This is Mom and Dad's room," she said.

"But I am in here and the door was closed," I said. "Don't ever walk into a room where the door is closed without knocking first, especially a bedroom or a bathroom."

"Can I come in?"

"No," I snarled. I couldn't even feel sorry for myself without her butting in.

"Are you crying?"

"Of course not. I'm an adult. Adults don't cry." I raised my head and looked at her haughtily, forgetting my bargain with fate. "Only little kids with runny noses cry. Once a person turns fifteen, their tear ducts dry up and they don't ever cry again."

"Mom cries," said Mandy.

"What?" I was surprised because my mother hardly ever cries. "Where did you get that idea?"

"I saw her. Just now." She frowned. "She was blowing her nose. She looked like she might cry."

"That's because she and Dad are arguing," I said. "And Mom's a softy. She hates arguments."

"They're arguing about me," said Mandy. "I got born and now they can't do anything they want."

"That's really dumb," I said scornfully. "You aren't that important."

"I am too. I heard her say that she doesn't know anybody to get to stay with us and that I'm too young to stay alone. Mom and Dad are fighting because of me."

"Let's go downstairs and ask them," I said, climbing to my feet. Get rid of Mandy and then I can go to my room and cry over Jerry in peace, I thought to myself. Probably right this very minute he's talking and laughing with Stephanie on the telephone.

Like everything else that evening, this little plan didn't work out either. By the time we reached the bottom of the stairs, we could hear our parents arguing. They were trying to keep their voices down, but they were arguing all right. I sat on the bottom step with Mandy to wait for a break in the hostilities.

"But I don't want to go to a dentists' convention," said Mom in a tired voice. She did sound as if she was going to

43

cry. "I have been to dentists' conventions, in Toledo three years ago, in Saint Paul a couple of years before that."

"It's important to keep up in the field," said Dad, retaining a comparative cool. "There are a lot of meetings on the convention agenda dealing with new techniques and materials. We've arranged for representatives to be present from all the major companies in dental supplies—"

"If you've seen one piece of dental floss, you've seen them all," said Mom with a flash of anger. "I can't see leaving our children alone so we can spend four days looking at Water Piks and mouthwash."

"But this convention is in Bermuda," yelled Dad, his voice suddenly going loud.

There was a short silence.

"Bermuda?" said Mom, her voice filled with wonder. "Did you say Bermuda?"

"Uh huh."

"I've never been to Bermuda," said Mom. "I've never been anywhere special."

"We could have a great time." Dad's voice was lower now. I figured this would be a good time to interrupt. I stood up.

"Oh, Harold. I don't know—"

"Rose and George already have their reservations in." Rose and George are their very closest friends. He's an orthodontist and they live on a farm where they raise Arabian horses. George straightened both Ron's and my teeth; my parents are always teasing him about the brood mare that the Witmers paid for.

"I don't know about leaving the girls."

"Allison is practically seventeen, for god's sake!"

"Not for four whole days, not in charge of Amanda."

"If Rose can leave with two mares with new foals—"

44

"Are you comparing our children with a couple of horses?"

"Those horses are worth an arm and a leg!"

"Harold Witmer—" All the pleasure was gone from Mom's voice. I grabbed Mandy's hand and dragged her back upstairs.

"Go to your room and look at comic books," I ordered. "I have to do my homework and I can't be interrupted."

"See! I told you it was my fault!" said Mandy. Tears glistened in her eyes. In a moment she would be howling.

I gritted my teeth. "It doesn't have anything to do with you," I said.

"It does! Mom said, 'Not in charge of Amanda.' If it was only you, they would go. Because of me, Mom has to stay home and they're fighting."

I flopped down on the cedar chest in the hall. Sitting on it, I was closer to her height.

"Listen to me," I said. "Do I ever lie to you?"

"Yes."

"Well, I'm not lying now. People fight all the time, big people, little people. You fight; I fight. Mom and Dad fight. It doesn't have a thing to do with you, not really. Do you understand?"

"Yes." There was a great relief in her blue eyes. She looked more like a five-year-old again instead of a worn and haggard age ten.

"Okay." I lightened my tone and made it very reasonable. "Now go to your room and look at comic books while I do my homework. After a while you can go downstairs and have your snack and watch television. All right?"

"All right." She didn't even hesitate. She went off to her room to browse through the pile of old comic books she keeps there.

I heaved a deep sigh. Then I went to my room and put the stereo on very low. I only wished my problems could be solved as easily as Amanda's.

On Hat Day I went to school as Tokyo Rose. I pinned a bright red cloth rose in my hair and used lots of eye shadow and blusher and bright red lipstick which exactly matched the rose. I also wore dark red nail polish and a black satiny blouse.

Two students in plane geometry wore top hats. One of them was Jerry; the other was a black kid named Tyrone Williams. They were standing together talking when I came into the room. Since they were both tall and by some coincidence both wore white shirts and dark pants that day, they looked like a pair of bookends.

"Hi," I told them in a voice I imagined Tokyo Rose would use. "Who are you guys supposed to be?"

"Abraham Lincoln," said Jerry. He didn't seem to notice

my eye shadow or my black blouse or even my red rose.

"You too?" I asked Tyrone.

"No." He grinned. "I'm Ralph Bunche, diplomat, UN Undersecretary General, winner of the Nobel Peace Prize."

"Oh."

"Who are you?"

"Tokyo Rose." My eyes followed Jerry as he went toward his seat. "She was a distant relation of mine."

"Sure," said Tyrone. "And your grandmother was a Chinese Eskimo."

For a minute I didn't need any blusher. My cheeks were red enough on their own. I slid a sidewise glance at Tyrone. He looked as if he might laugh any second.

"Catch you later," I told him and followed Jerry.

Jerry did look very good in a top hat. It made him seem even taller and set off his lean features and his gray eyes. I spent most of plane geometry drooling over him when I was supposed to be doing serious work with numbers.

Mr. Garner left the room a couple of minutes before the period was over to pick up some papers in the office. I turned to Jerry and lowered my lashes, then raised them slowly and turned on all my fatal charm.

He gave me a confused smile.

Hans swiveled in his seat.

"Ave, Allison," he said. He had gone all out. He was wearing one of the Favazzos' bed sheets and had a wreath of green leaves on his head. It had slipped to one side, giving him the look of a slightly drunken Ku Klux Klanner.

"Hail, Caesar," said Jerry, forgetting about me.

"Ave, man, ave," said Hans. "You have to speak the language, or you won't get any pizza."

I gave Hans a very searing look. It told him to drop dead or to shut up, to do anything, but get out of Jerry's and my life.

"You are one sexy lady today," he said, not getting the message.

I forgave him.

"Who are you supposed to be?" asked Jerry, finally looking at me as if I wasn't a part of the wall or the chalkboard.

"Tokyo Rose." I made my eyes cloudy and mysterious.

"Who is sweet Celia?" Hans looked so pathetic that I took pity on him.

"Meet us at our lockers after lunch," I said, "and you can see for yourself."

"Thanks!" As the bell rang, he was up and off in a swirl of bed sheets.

"I want to talk with you alone," said Jerry. "Try to get to lit. class early."

My legs seemed to melt. I had to sit down again while I gathered my books for my next class. Jerry wanted to talk to me alone. To me! It wasn't exactly the same as asking me to marry him, but it was the first step.

I was so excited about Jerry's wanting to meet me in literature class that nothing bothered me that day, not even the sight of Stephanie wearing a nurse's cap, her golden red curls tumbling about it in glorious beauty. I gave her a dazzling smile.

I wanted to tell Celia my thrilling news over lunch, but I didn't have a chance. We sat at a table with five boys, and they all talked to her and didn't say a word to me. That didn't surprise me one bit. Celia had come to school in Cleopatra's hat, or crown, I should say. It was made of braided gold wire, the front twisted up into a snake with red jeweled eyes. Celia's black hair was sleek and smooth, her eyes outlined in black liner with silver and turquoise eye shadow. Her lashes were long and curved and black.

What did I care about Stephanie's reddish blond beauty, that overnight Celia had turned into a sultry temptress from

Egypt? What did I care that I was practically isolated at a table full of boys watching Celia and ignoring me? I had my dreams, all of them centered on Jerry. He wanted to talk to me. I sure was grateful to Tokyo Rose.

I trailed Celia out of the cafeteria and to our lockers, where I waited patiently as she fumbled with her lock and exchanged books and notebooks. I was just about to tell her about Jerry when Hans appeared, his bed sheet dragging behind him.

"Hi, Allison," he said, watching Celia. "Hello, sweet Celia."

Celia rolled her eyes at the ceiling.

"She is the light of my life," said Hans dramatically. He put his right hand on the sheet, somewhere over his heart. "She sings, she sways, she glows in the dark."

"Cut it out," said Celia.

"For you." He plucked the wreath of leaves from his head and gave it to her.

"What would I want with this?" Celia stared at the limp dangling bunch of leaves.

"Put it on your pillow at night. Dream of me, little turtledove," said Hans.

"It looks buggy." She shoved the wreath back at him. "Good-bye, Hans. Allison wants to talk with me."

Hans stood for a second, a hurt expression on his face, the bunch of leaves in his hand. Then he went off down the hall.

"I think he likes you," I told Celia.

"Hans?"

"Yes. I know he'd sit with us at lunch if you were nicer to him."

"He's a clown," she said. "You'd think he'd pick up a little polish from Lee. What did you want to tell me?"

"Jerry wants me to meet him before literature class."

"Really?"

"For sure. I'll tell you about it after school," I promised, as I edged away, headed toward my next class.

From research, I know exactly where all of Jerry's classes are each period of the day. From research, I even know which chair he sits in in which room. I know that the sun is in his eyes in Spanish and that he is next to the chalkboard in history. I do not know which locker he uses for gym, because I have never been in the boys' locker room, but I am working on it.

The point is that Jerry has Spanish right next door to literature and can go from one room to the other in ten seconds flat. I am in study hall, a long two halls away and down one floor. To get to literature early, I was going to have to hustle.

For a World War II spy, it was nothing. Spies have to be in good shape. They do a lot of running from bullets and speeding cars. It is all a matter of timing.

I gathered my books together in my arms five minutes before the study hall ended. I did deep breathing in the last two minutes to hyperventilate for extra oxygen and then gathered my feet under me, ready for action.

The bell rang. I shot out of my chair, out the door, and down the hall. Classes were only beginning to empty as I reached the stairs, sped up them two at a time, and headed down the second corridor.

"Hey!" yelled a hall monitor.

I ignored him. By this time the crowd was growing, but twisting sideways and using my right shoulder as a wedge, I forced myself along at a good rate. I was right behind Jerry when he strolled into literature.

We were alone.

"Hi," said Jerry. "Thanks for hurrying."

"It was nothing," I panted. I patted my rose to make certain it was still in my hair.

"I wanted to ask you something."

"Yes?"

"Do you think that Stephanie is interested in me, or do you think she's only trying not to hurt my feelings?"

I couldn't think of a thing to say. I just stared at him. Then I slowly sank into my seat. Jerry sat down behind me, leaning forward in a tense silence as if his whole future hinged on my answer.

"I called her the other night, the way you told me to."

"Congratulations."

"She was real nice on the phone."

"I am happy for you."

"Anyway, I asked her to go to the movies Friday night."

I swallowed twice. Realism time, I told myself. Face it, Allison, this guy is not interested in you. Then I spent a couple of seconds trying not to cry. Crying would only make my makeup run, make a fool of me, and probably frighten Jerry.

He was still talking, some garbage about what he said, then what Stephanie said, and then what he said again, as if I wanted to listen in on their private love life.

"She said she'd let me know," he finished, a bewildered expression on his face. "She said that maybe her parents might have something planned, that she'd have to talk to them. Then I asked her again today and she said she still doesn't know."

Stephanie Harris should be strung up by her thumbs, I thought. She should be given twenty lashes with a whip.

"What kind of an answer is that?" asked Jerry, his face darkening.

"Maybe it's the truth," I said dully. "Maybe her parents won't tell her their plans ahead of time."

"You think?"

"It could be a difficult situation for her." I felt as if I were far away, in a different world. My whole self, my soul included, felt numb. It was the shock, I decided. My senses were trying to protect me. Only later would I feel the searing pain of unrequited love.

Jerry sighed. "I don't know," he said. "Somehow I think she should be a little more enthusiastic."

"So do I," I said. "She should have leapt at the chance. She should have said, 'Jerry, I would love to go to the movies with you.'"

"Are you teasing me?"

"Absolutely not," I said flatly.

Jerry frowned, considering this. Then he said, "Did you know that Tokyo Rose was not really a spy, that she put on radio broadcasts trying to get our men to desert?"

"I thought she was an American spy in Japan," I said.

"No. She was on the other side."

"The other side," I repeated stupidly.

"Don't worry about it. There isn't any reason for you to know about spies."

"Listen." I gave a quick glance around the room, which was beginning to fill with students. I leaned my head close to Jerry's. "I shouldn't tell you this, but my father is a spy."

"What?"

"CIA." I nodded, keeping my voice down.

"Where?" Jerry's gray eyes were shocked.

"I don't know where. Neither does my mother. He goes away on these trips that last from two weeks to a month. We don't know where he is, but my mother has a number in Washington to call if there is ever bad trouble at home. A government man watches our house day and night while he's gone."

"Wow," said Jerry. "Aren't you scared?"

"No." I shrugged. "I used to be when I was a little kid, but I'm used to it now."

"Gee. My dad's only a sales representative," said Jerry. He looked at me with new respect.

I turned around in my seat. I should have felt rotten telling Jerry that my dad was a spy, but I didn't. I didn't even care. And I didn't regret it, not one little bit.

8

Once I started making up fascinating facts about the Witmer family, it seemed I couldn't stop. Not only did I tell Jerry that my dad was a spy, but somehow within the next few days I also told him that my mother was Miss Tennessee, that I owned a pet monkey named Alfred, and that I had been bitten by a rabid dog as a small child but had survived.

Jerry took all this in with increasing amazement. He stopped asking my advice about his love life. He brought Stephanie up only once, and that was in geometry class.

"Do you think Stephanie—" he began.

"Jerry, will you do me a big favor?" I blurted. My voice was extra loud and I sounded mad. I didn't care that Fran Wilson was listening again. This time Fran was going to hear the truth.

Hans turned around in his seat, eyeing us silently, looking like a spanked puppy. It occurred to me that he had been very quiet ever since Celia handed back his laurel wreath.

"What?" Jerry was so startled that he didn't finish his sentence.

"Just don't tell me about you and Stephanie."

"But—"

"I don't want to hear about it," I said nastily.

"I thought you were interested," said Jerry. "I thought you were my buddy."

"I don't want to be your buddy!" I howled, and buried my head in my geometry book.

"It's this wind that has been blowing," said Hans to Jerry. "For three days it blows. In France they have a name for a wind like this. It is called the mistral. It drives everyone a little crazy."

"She's a little crazy all right," said Jerry. "She's been strange all week. Now she's acting as if she can't stand the sight of me."

I raised my head to glare at him. "It isn't you, Jerry," I said. "Normally I like you a lot, very much. It is your infatuation with this girl who isn't interested in you that gets me down. I don't ever want to talk about it again."

Jerry went sort of pale and his mouth came together in a thin line. He looked away from me and he didn't look back. He didn't glance at me in literature class seventh period either.

Good, I thought. At least I didn't have to advise him on his love life.

Celia had been excused from school that day to go with her father to her grandparents in Michigan for a long weekend. It was her grandparents' golden wedding anniversary, and all their family was getting together to celebrate. Celia said she didn't mind going to Michigan and seeing her relatives, but she hated to miss her belly-dancing class. She said they were getting to the interesting part.

It was almost a relief to go home that afternoon and not have to face school until Monday. It was a lot easier to deal with Amanda and my parents instead of sitting in class and witnessing Jerry's love life and Hans' broken heart and Celia's infatuation with Lee. At least my parents tolerated me, and it was obvious that Mandy adored me. A little adoration never hurt anyone, not even from a kid sister.

Mom was busy in the kitchen, making a batch of soft pretzels. Cooking is her hobby and baking is what she does best. She says she likes to bake while she thinks because it keeps her hands busy and her mind free for other things. Lately she has been thinking a lot. I've gained three pounds but Mandy is still skinny.

"I've been wanting to talk with you," she said right away. She put the dough into a big bowl and covered it with a towel to rise. It would be hours before the pretzels would be ready to bake.

"Yes," I said. I didn't think I'd done anything wrong, not that she knew about anyway.

"Do you think you would be able to take care of Amanda if your father and I went to Bermuda?"

"You're going!"

"I didn't say that, and don't you tell your father." She smiled. She might not be Miss Tennessee, but she does have a beautiful smile. "But he wants to go, and to tell the truth, I wouldn't mind a vacation either."

Neither would I, I thought to myself. Out loud I said, "Of course I can. A lot of girls my age have their own kids."

That shook her up a little. "I can always get Ron to come home from college for the weekend," she said. "I ought to call him anyway. He hasn't written a letter in weeks."

"I can take care of it, Mom. Ron doesn't have to come home."

"Well, I'll have to think about it." She patted the bowl full of dough reflectively. "Go get Mandy, will you? I think she's out in that tree house and she's catching another cold."

Acting the good daughter, I trotted off in the direction of the tree house which is at the Morgans', our next-door neighbors. At least we call them that, since they are the next neighbors to the north of our house. They spend a large part of the year in Florida, coming home only in the summer time.

Their place must have been very nice once, sort of like a park with trees and shrubbery, but now the trees have grown together, and from long neglect the shrubs are wild and tangled.

The tree house is a leftover from the time the property swarmed with mutts and kids. It is in the center of a little grove of trees, four feet off the ground. There are weathered wood walls on three sides and a slanted roof, complete with rotting shingles. I don't think it's a good place to play because it's isolated. When I was a kid, I never played there because I was afraid of strangers with sacks of candy after little girls, but Mandy is not the fraidycat I was.

"Hey you." I knocked on the side of the weathered boards as I came around to the opening. "Come out of that tree."

"What for?" Mandy was sitting with crossed legs like an Indian, a hand on each knobby knee. She was catching a cold all right. Her nose was running.

"Mom wants you."

"This is my private place," said Mandy with great dignity. "You should ask before you come in."

"At least I knocked." I glanced around at the tangled undergrowth, the stand of trees. "I don't see why you have to play here."

"I like it."

I studied her. "Do you know," I began and waited to get her interest, "that this is a very dangerous spot?"

"Is not."

"It is too," I said coolly. "This is a magic tree house. If a person sits in it too often, that person will turn into a horrible warty little toad and hop away and have to live under rocks."

"I like toads."

"They eat flies and ants and mosquitoes," I said.

"Besides, that isn't true," she said. "I've been here lots and I'm no toad."

"Have you looked in the mirror lately?"

"Allison!"

"Come on," I ordered. "Mom wants you."

She didn't move.

"Come on, Mandy." My patience was wearing thin.

"Oh, all right." She dropped to the ground. "I hate *Mandy*," she said. "It reminds me of a panda."

"Mandy Pandy," I called her.

"I *hate* pandas," she said, her face taking on a stubborn expression.

"Do you know what they are?"

"Bears," she said. "Ugly stinking bears."

I was shocked. "They are not ugly. They're beautiful with ebony black and snowy white fur. They have white heads with round black ears and black circles around their eyes."

"Yeah." She looked happier.

"But of course they do smell awful," I added. I couldn't help myself. "Sort of like an elementary school child."

By the time we were back at the house, Mom was waiting with the phone in one hand and the thermometer in the other. I took the phone and waited until she and Amanda went into another room to play nurse.

59

"Hello," I said. I thought it was Mrs. Owens. She had been nagging me to baby-sit her boys the night of May fifth. That is the night of the prom, but also the night of the Elks' ball and some big event at the Country Club. Parents were going berserk trying to get sitters, and most of the sitters were planning to go to the dance, or hoping to anyway.

It wasn't Mrs. Owens. It was Celia.

"I thought you were in Michigan!" I said.

"I am."

"You're calling me from Michigan?"

"Yeah."

"Your grandparents don't care?" I had visions of dollar bills disappearing into the phone.

"They don't know. Everybody's downstairs yakking at each other." There was a slight pause. "Listen. I want to read you something. It came in the mail this morning before we left home."

"I'm listening."

Over the line I could hear her take a deep breath.

" 'Song, To Celia,' by Ben Jonson, second verse," she read.

> "I sent thee late a rosy wreath,
>   Not so much honoring thee
> As giving it a hope, that there
>   It could not withered be;
> But thou thereon didst only breathe,
>   And sent'st it back to me;
> Since when it grows, and smells, I swear,
>   Not of itself but thee."

There was a silence filled with her breathing. I could hear it plain as if we were in the same room. Better.

"Isn't that the most romantic thing you ever heard of?" she

60

asked. "The word *rosy* is crossed out, and *laurel* is written in above it."

"Hans wrote that?"

"No, Ben Jonson wrote it, stupid. Hans copied it."

"Can't Hans get in trouble that way?"

"Allison!" She sounded very irritated with me. "Isn't it romantic?"

"It's romantic," I said hurriedly.

"Now I have two boys interested in me."

"Who is the other one?"

"Lee."

"Since when?"

The phone crackled. I think maybe it was with the force of her anger. She was probably trying to send me lightning bolts down the line.

"Is there something you aren't telling me?" I asked, trying to make things better between us.

"Of course not," she exploded. "It's only that I didn't call you all the way from Michigan to be insulted."

"I'm not insulting you. I think it's very romantic. I think Hans is a great guy, and he is very interested in you. He's been depressed all week. I think his heart is breaking from unrequited love."

"Really?"

"Really," I said.

"He is sort of cute," said Celia. "But not as cute as Lee."

"But much more romantic," I pointed out. "I don't think Lee knows much about poetry."

Celia didn't answer me. I could hear conversation in the background. Then she came back on the phone.

"I've got to run," she said. "My grandmother wants to know who I'm talking to. See you Monday."

Mom poured on the tender loving care with Mandy, and Mandy's cold improved almost overnight. Pouring on the tender loving care meant lots of vitamin C tablets, orange juice, and back rubs. I don't know how back rubs help a cold, but it is almost worth being sick to have one.

By Sunday noon, Mandy was running around minus a cough and a stuffed-up nose, and Mom had reached the point where she was willing to admit that going to Bermuda might be a possibility. We were sitting around the table in the midst of our dirty lunch dishes. It was raining as usual. It had been raining off and on for a week.

"Does it rain in Bermuda this time of year?" asked Mom.

"Never," said Dad. "Absolutely guaranteed, no rain."

"When is this convention scheduled for?" she asked tentatively.

"The first weekend in May." He tried to act casual, but he didn't pull it off. His eyes were too eager.

"Why that's hardly any time at all," said Mom, disappointment mixing with relief in her tones. "It must be too late for reservations."

"They, er—they had to be made in November."

"But—" Mom's brown eyes looked puzzled, then aware, then angry. "Harold Witmer, you sent in the reservations without asking me!"

"It was to be a surprise."

"Some surprise!"

"An early wedding anniversary present," he said. "I knew you'd love it." He looked at her and said softly, "We could have a terrific time together."

"Well—"

"White sandy beaches, string bands playing, the sea."

She made a noise deep in her throat.

"Remember back before Mandy was born," he said, "when we talked about how nice it was that you didn't have to work outside the home, didn't want to? How when the kids got older we would be free to go places together, travel? This is our first trip."

Mom smiled. She glanced at her plate, at the bouquet of yellow and white daffodils in the center of the table, then at Dad.

"Can I have a dog?" said Mandy.

They both looked at her, their minds elsewhere.

"Allison had one," Mandy said.

"What about Bermuda?" asked Dad.

"We'll go."

"Whoopee!" He jumped out of his chair and did a little dance. Then he grabbed her and kissed her.

"A girl in my kindergarten has a Saint Bernard and it had puppies," said Amanda.

"We'll have to make plans," said Mom. "Maybe I should call Ron and see if he can come home to be with the girls that weekend."

"We can stay by ourselves," I said.

"But I *want* a dog," said Mandy.

"Listen, Allison," said Dad. "You mother and I have things to talk about. Why don't you take Mandy and go to the movies?"

"In the afternoon? That's for little kids."

"So she's a little kid and you're taking her."

"I want to go to the movies!" said Mandy, the Saint Bernard temporarily forgotten.

"Go on. It will get you out of the house. You've been stuck in here all weekend."

We went to the movies. There were only two matinees. The first one was showing a double feature, *Sex Sirens of Saturn* and *The Return of the Marquis de Sade,* both rated R. The Golden Oldie Theatre was running a Charlie Chaplin film festival, which included parts of his most famous movies. We went to the Charlie Chaplin film festival, arriving after it had started.

Charlie Chaplin was very funny. He had a derby and a cane and he walked with his toes pointed out in different directions. He had on a lot of white makeup, or maybe it was the old film, but his eyes seemed very large and dark in his pale face. He didn't need any words. The expressions on his face were enough to make Amanda and me laugh until our sides ached.

The part of the film I liked best was from a movie made in Alaska. Charlie fell in love and followed a woman to her shack. Then he was caught in a cabin in an avalanche. The cabin kept teetering back and forth on the edge of a precipice while a huge menacing man tried to catch Charlie. Charlie kept sliding down the floor and crawling up to the door to

64

try to get out and escape. I laughed until I forgot I was at the movies with my little sister, that I was entangling myself in lies, and that Jerry thought I was acting crazy. I laughed so hard my eyes teared, and I had to blow my nose on the napkin I got with my popcorn since I didn't have any tissues with me.

"Come on," I said to Mandy when the lights flickered back on. "Let's walk home instead of calling Dad."

"I'm hungry," she whined.

"We'll buy a couple of candy bars."

"Okay." She held her right arm out, imaginary cane at her side, pointed her toes east and west, and waddled up the aisle like Charlie Chaplin. I followed, happier than I had been in days.

There wasn't anyone in line at the refreshment stand, but the guy behind the counter was looking at *Playboy* and pretended not to see me.

I stood and waited while Amanda hustled around the lobby acting like Charlie Chaplin.

"I didn't know you liked old movies," came a voice from behind me. "You never say anything about them."

Jerry! Adrenaline rushed through my body.

"I never saw one before," I said. I decided on complete honesty. No more trying to trap him, no sexy mysterious smiles and fluttering my eyelashes to get his attention. If I couldn't be his girlfriend, I would settle for being his buddy.

Jerry edged around us to lean on the counter, Hans at his elbow, just like in geometry.

"What do you think of Chaplin?" he asked.

"He's so funny!" I thought of Charlie making a pass at the girl in the movie and started to giggle.

"Don't lean on the counter," said the guy, dropping his *Playboy*.

"I'll have two Hershey bars and a Peanut Butter Cup," I said loudly.

He gave a disgusted snort and managed to get to his feet, give me the candy, and take my money. He glared at Jerry until Jerry took his elbow off the counter.

"Where's my little turtledove?" asked Hans, looking around as if he expected to find Celia hiding behind the popcorn machine.

"She flew to Michigan for the weekend."

"Oh." He looked desolate. "When did she leave?"

"Right after she received your poem. She liked it."

"Whewee!" Hans waved his arms like wings.

Mandy passed by us again, walking like Charlie Chaplin. Hans fell in behind, imitating her imitating Chaplin. They looked like a couple of large mechanical dolls.

"Chaplin is the greatest silent-film star of all time," said Jerry, a reverent note in his voice. "It's too bad, but this theater doesn't show many of his movies. People won't turn out for Chaplin."

"Maybe that's because they've never seen him," I said. We moved slowly toward the big double doors, Amanda and Hans following like a parade.

"There was a good crowd last month for W. C. Fields, and a lot of people two weeks ago for *High Noon*," said Jerry. "People like Westerns."

"I didn't know old movies could be so much fun," I said. "They're a lot better in the theater than they are on television."

We stepped outside the doors. The late afternoon was warm and it had stopped raining. The air was fresh. A little breeze blew, lifting my hair, smelling of spring.

Jerry leaned against the front wall of the theater. He gazed down at me as if he were really seeing me for a change. "Did you do something to your eyes?" he asked. "They look different."

"Probably from the dark," I said. I hadn't worn any eye shadow or mascara.

"You should be in the dark more often," he said. Then he looked embarrassed.

I considered lowering my eyelashes and peering up at him from under them, but I restrained myself.

Amanda was still doing her Chaplin thing. Maybe it would become a habit. Then my parents would have something else to think about besides Bermuda.

Hans was taking off an imaginary hat and bowing low to passersby. The passersby were giving him odd glances. An old lady stepped off the sidewalk into the street in order to get farther from him.

"See you tomorrow," said Jerry.

I don't know what I said. All I know is I went the opposite direction with Mandy, who was still walking like Chaplin. I handed her one of the Hershey bars and started unwrapping the other one for myself. I was saving the Peanut Butter Cup for later.

"It's all melted," she complained.

"From my hot little hands," I told her. "Warm hands, warm heart."

"Who was that guy?" she demanded, her mouth full of chocolate.

"Prince Charming," I said. "He's going to sweep me up on his white charger and take me away to live in a castle."

"What's a charger?"

"A horse, dummy."

"Will you fight a lot?"

"Never. Hardly ever."

67

"Can I live with you?"

I was in a generous mood. "If you promise to take out the garbage and don't play in the moat," I told her.

10

The next day I went to school disguised as myself. I wore my most comfortable pair of jeans and my old blue top, the one that is sky blue and makes my eyes look darker brown. I didn't wear any mascara, or carry a rose or a tennis racket. I didn't wiggle my hips or flutter my eyelashes or make my voice low and sexy. I felt very strange, sort of free.

I had made a firm resolution to myself on the bus. From now on, no matter what, Jerry and I were going to be friends. I would be my own natural, uninteresting self, the nice girl with the pointy chin. I would keep my dreams and fantasies about Jerry under control, apart from reality. I would be Jerry's buddy. I would even listen to his love life if he wanted to tell me about it.

Celia and I skipped the bus after school that day and

walked to her house. After all the rain, it was warm and sunny, the grass was a fresh green, and the trees were beginning to show the first signs of leaves. Celia told me all about her grandparents' anniversary and about her cousins and how much fun she'd had in Michigan.

She was still talking about it after we got to her house, while she opened the curtains in her room, threw her books on the unmade bed, and shuffled through her records. She picked out the one with the belly-dancing music and put it on. I sat on the floor in front of her dresser and watched her.

Celia didn't seem to notice how quiet I was. She took a bottle of Spunsugar nail polish from her dresser and sat at her desk to do her nails. I regarded her gloomily. Here I was, a new quiet, mature, and reserved me, and my best friend didn't even notice. All she could think of was to paint her nails a different color.

The phone in her dad's bedroom began to ring.

"Answer it, will you?" she said, concentrating on the little finger of her right hand.

"You get it," I protested. I didn't like going into her dad's room. I felt like a trespasser.

"Get it! You want me to smear nail polish all over everything?"

The phone stopped for about ten seconds and then began ringing again.

Celia jumped to her feet and knocked over the bottle of nail polish.

While she stood staring at the little pink river crossing her desk top, I ran to answer the phone.

"Hi," I said, out of breath. Mr. Myers' bedroom was dark and smelled of after-shave. There was a striped necktie draped over a chair by the window and a pile of paperback books on the floor by the bed.

70

"Celia, this is Lee—"

"Lee!"

"Lee Favazzo," he said, as if any girl in the radius of ten miles wouldn't know of Lee Favazzo.

"This isn't Celia," I said rapidly. "It's Allison. Hang on. I'll get her."

I raced back to Celia's room. She was mopping up the nail polish.

"It's Lee Favazzo!" I shouted.

"Sure." She twisted her lips and narrowed her eyes at me. "I paid five dollars for that nail polish."

"Celia, it really is Lee," I breathed.

Her eyes went huge and she stopped all movement.

"He's on the phone. I told him I'd get you."

"Lee Favazzo?" She sat down on her desk chair, staring blankly ahead of her.

"He's on the phone."

She didn't move. I started hopping from foot to foot. She looked at me.

"Come on," I said, grabbing her arm.

"I can't. What will I say?"

"Nothing. Anything." I dragged her into the other room and shoved the receiver into her hand. She held it down at her side, then raised her head slowly like Joan of Arc facing an uncertain future, and put the receiver to her mouth.

"Hello," she said into the earpiece.

Lee started talking but I couldn't hear more than the first couple of words because after that Celia had the phone in the right position.

"Yes," said Celia. "Yes." She looked a little confused. Then she smiled and said, "I'd love to."

I was holding my breath. I didn't realize it until I almost

passed out. By that time Celia had hung up the phone and was headed back to her room. I chased after her, begging to know what Lee had said. She ignored me.

"If you don't tell me this instant, I'm going home and will never speak to you again!" I yelled.

"He asked me to the dance," she said.

Miracles really do happen.

I sat down abruptly.

"He asked me for Hans."

"What?"

"Hans is so shy and sweet. He was afraid to ask me for himself. He was afraid I wouldn't go." Celia smiled. "Isn't that ridiculous?"

"I thought you didn't like Hans. You said he was a clown. You're going to the prom with a clown." I shouldn't have said that. I should have been glad for Hans and Celia, but I was sick with jealousy. Now I wouldn't have Celia to comfort me in my misery. I would be sitting home the night of the prom alone, while Celia was off dancing with Hans.

"Hey," said Celia, "to get to that dance, I'd go with Jack the Ripper."

"Hans is a nice guy," I said, trying to make up for calling him a clown. "I like him better than Lee."

"European men are so smooth, so sophisticated," said Celia.

"Hans? Smooth?"

"Of course." She frowned, knitting her black eyebrows. "Haven't you noticed?" She sat down in her desk chair and played with the bottle of Spunsugar, forgetting that only the nails on her right hand were polished.

"No."

"Do you know what his middle name is?"

I had to admit I didn't.

72

"Wolfgang. Isn't that the most romantic name you've ever heard of? Hans Wolfgang Spengler."

It could have been worse. It could have been Adolph. "I guess so," I said. A vision of a gang of wolves with dark soulful eyes and grins like Hans' filled my mind.

"We're going to double-date with Lee and Missy," said Celia. Then she laughed. "You know what? I really am going to the dance with Lee, at least in his car. Only my date is with Hans."

"You'll have a great time," I said. I was having trouble sounding cheerful. I decided I had better accept that baby-sitting job with Mrs. Owens. I might as well get used to baby-sitting while other kids went out and had all the fun.

"Hey," said Celia. "You'll go with Jerry. I know you will."

"Uh-uh." I shook my head. "He won't ask me. Besides, I told him so much stuff about myself and my family that I'd actually be afraid to go out with him now. If he ever finds out all those stories aren't true, he's going to hate me."

"What did you tell him?"

"Stuff about my dad and my mom and me."

"Like what?"

"Like I'm practically a professional tennis player and that I was once bitten by a rabid dog and I have a pet monkey."

Celia was appalled. "You can always buy a monkey," she said, "but you could never pull off playing tennis."

"I also told him my mother was Miss Tennessee."

"But Allison, that's a joke! All he has to do is see her once!"

"It seemed like the truth at the time," I said gloomily.

"I mean she is practically a dwarf."

"So what do you have against little people?"

"Nothing."

"Anyway," I sighed, "I can dream about Jerry, but I can't have him. From now on, I'm going to school as me. I'll study hard, make good grades, and get a good job with a decent pension plan when I graduate from college."

It was plain that Celia didn't believe me. I meant every word though. The next day I wore the same blue jeans with a different blouse to school. I also wore a gold bracelet, but I figured even girls who are plain and without personality deserve a little decoration now and then.

I didn't have to worry about talking with Jerry in geometry. Hans was so excited about his date with Celia that he didn't even shut up when Mr. Garner came in and started class. Mr. Garner had to tell him three times to be quiet and finally told Hans he would get two detentions if he said another word.

I didn't have to worry about talking with Jerry in literature either. I was late for class. Jerry looked up and smiled as I slid into my seat in front of him. I listened carefully to Mrs. Groves and the lesson. Poetry wasn't all that strange and difficult when I put my mind to it.

As my new competent, serious self, I was very organized. When the dismissal bell rang, I gathered my books as I rose and quietly and efficiently left the room. In seconds I was dodging through bodies in the crowded halls.

"Wait, will you?" said Jerry, catching up with me, grabbing my arm and almost making me drop my books. "Most days you hang around that room like you don't know which way is home. Today you're off like a track star."

I listened patiently. In my life many people would come to me for advice; none for love.

"I think it's terrific you like old movies," said Jerry.

"Thank you."

"Because I like old movies."

74

"That's nice." Celia would be waiting. We would miss the bus and it was raining again.

"Will you go to the dance with me?" asked Jerry.

"Huh?"

"Will you go to the prom with me?" he repeated slowly, as if I were hard of hearing or a little slow in my mental processes.

"Why?" Yikes! Was that smooth! "I mean, I thought you asked Stephanie," I managed, then cursed myself.

"No, I did not ask Stephanie," said Jerry, still speaking very slowly. "I decided that Stephanie is a very nice girl, but I am not interested in her."

"Oh," I managed. My brain was having a little trouble adjusting. "You decided to ask your old buddy?"

Jerry leaned way over at me. He looked directly into my eyes from a distance of about three inches. I looked back. Some part of me registered that he had tiny flecks of blue mixed into the gray of his eyes, while another part of me noted the heavy thumping of my heart and wondered if Jerry could hear it.

"Has it ever occurred to you," he asked softly, "that we could be more than buddies?"

11

Mom was almost as excited about my date to the prom as I was. The big difference was that she was excited that I was going to the dance; I was excited to be going out with Jerry. I would go anywhere with Jerry, to the snake-infested jungles of the Amazon if he asked me.

She called Ron right away that evening and made arrangements for him to come home the day of the dance. Then Mom spent so much time asking him about college that I didn't even get a chance to say hello. That was all right. Ron and I could talk lots over the weekend.

Mom decided that she and I should spend all of Saturday shopping for clothes. Shopping trips are nothing new. We always spend a day shopping in August before school begins, and only last fall we had gone out on a special trip looking for a dress for me for the Homecoming Dance. Usually we have a lot of fun, poking around in stores and eating lunch together, and then poking around in stores again.

I thought that shopping for a gown for the prom would be exactly like shopping for a dress for the Homecoming Dance. Was I ever wrong. In the first place, I hadn't much cared what I wore to Homecoming since George Reese was my date. I had absolutely no desire to be overly attractive to George, but I sure did want to be super attractive to Jerry. Also, since the prom was rapidly approaching, that Saturday was the only day I had to find something. The dress I had bought for Homecoming just wasn't formal enough.

To further complicate matters, Mom had to find a white tennis outfit to take to Bermuda. Mom didn't care about tennis on the trip, but my dad wanted to play, and she was determined not to do one thing to ruin his good time. I insisted we pick up her tennis dress first. Then we would have the rest of the day to concentrate on my gown.

It is not easy to find a white tennis dress in size 20.

We went to four stores and then we ended up in The Speciality Sports Shoppe.

Mom went straight to a rack of tops near the front of the store.

"You have to get your clothes for tennis," I reminded.

"I had forgotten they have such nice things in here," she said, pulling an embroidered top from the rack. "Oh, Allison, look at this. It's your size too. Try it on."

"First we look at tennis dresses."

Mom sighed. She didn't put the top back. Instead, she draped it over one arm while we went to look at the tennis dresses.

The Shoppe had four in size 20. Two were light blue, one was flamingo pink, and one was white. The white one was the shortest.

"I don't see why we have to wear white on the courts,"

said Mom. "We're supposed to be there for a good time. Why can't we wear what we want?"

"Probably something to do with the glamour of Bermuda," I pointed out. "The folder from your hotel said it was the same everywhere—white on tennis courts."

Even with the rules, it took me ten minutes to talk Mom into putting on the dress.

It didn't do a whole lot for her figure.

"It looks like the ruffled plastic panties I used to put on you and Mandy when you were babies," she observed, seeing herself in the mirror.

"Everyone wears tennis skirts and panties, Mom. Your friends have been wearing them for years."

"Their legs are thinner than mine." She twisted and turned before the mirror, tugging at the bottom of the skirt, then at the panties. "Maybe I could find a pair of white culottes."

I sighed. It was almost noon, and we hadn't looked at a single gown for me.

"When are we going to look for a dress for the dance?" I asked.

"Aren't there any in here?" She glanced around, still distraught over her short skirt.

"The Speciality Sports Shoppe?"

"Tell you what." She smiled suddenly. "You charge these things while I put some clothes on. We'll go for lunch, and then we'll go shopping for a gown for you. There must be dozens of beautiful dresses just waiting to be tried on."

That sounded like a good plan. The lunch part turned out perfectly fine, with fried clams, french fries, and a strawberry shake. The rest of the day was not an experience I would ever care to repeat. It was a total disaster.

Mom and I had completely different ideas of what was a beautiful dress for the prom. I had in mind something simple but sensational, understated and sophisticated, maybe in black or in a long slender white. I could pile my hair high on my head and wear the highest heels possible. Jerry would take one look at me and go completely out of his mind, but not so completely that we didn't make it to the dance. At the dance the boys would stare at me in open admiration and the girls would grind their teeth in frustration and jealousy.

I think my mother wanted me to look a lot like the Shirley Temple doll that Aunt Joy had given me. I love the doll; it is one of my most precious possessions. I think that Shirley Temple was a great actress and the doll's dress is sweet, long and fluffy, perfect for a Southern belle. I am not the Southern belle type; I am more cosmopolitan and worldly.

I wanted to look sultry and suggestive. I wanted a gown that was sleek and elegant and sensual. I wanted Jerry to realize that I am a mature and passionate woman.

"You'd have to be at least thirty to wear that dress!" Mom said when I finally pulled one off a rack.

I held it against me. It was black and shiny, cut very low in the front and even lower in the back, with spaghetti straps.

"And have a police escort," she added.

"I'll just try it on."

"No."

"But Mom—"

"I said no, Allison!"

I put the dress back on the rack. I swallowed the lump in my throat while I browsed through the rest of the dresses. Not one of them looked like me.

"Here." Mom pulled out something big and ruffled and covered with tiers of some limp yellow material.

"Nobody wears dresses like that," I said.

"I think it's perfectly beautiful, so springlike, so like a fresh young girl."

I took the thing in my hands. It was built way out in the

bust, with stays to hold the dress's shape. I might be big on top, but I am not that big.

"What if Jerry hugs me?" I asked. "He'll leave big dents in my front."

"He doesn't need to hug you. You are going to a dance, not to a crushing contest."

"But Mom, I could never fill that. Not even Dolly Parton could fill that!"

She pressed her lips together in a straight line, looked at the dress one more time, and shoved it back onto the rack.

"I didn't know you were going to be so difficult," she said.

"I'm not being difficult. I am only trying to find a dress I like." I was hot and tired. I decided I hated both the perfumed atmosphere of ladies' stores and the soft gentle music piped through the sound system.

"I always thought that Amanda was the obstinate one."

Our voices were rising. Three clerks turned their heads in our direction. The older ones gave Mom sympathetic looks. The youngest smiled at me.

We went to three more stores. My head ached, my feet ached, and my stomach ached. I decided never again to eat fried clams for lunch. I also decided never again to agree to go shopping with my mother.

My mother was pale and haggard. Her new hairstyle was flat, and all her makeup had worn off. She looked as if she had a headache too. I didn't ask. I wasn't feeling up to conversation.

The last store we went to had what Mom called a helpful clerk. That meant that the clerk agreed with everything Mom said. She agreed that I was young and inexperienced and a little simpleminded when it came to choosing formal clothes. She agreed that the prom was a very important event and that I needed a dress that I could remember in future years as a symbol of my fresh and innocent youth. She also agreed that the light blue dress with the wide dark blue sash and the off-the-shoulder sleeves that Mom picked out was absolutely perfect for me.

I stood in front of the triple mirror on the plush carpet with Mom and the clerk standing grinning behind me.

"I look awful," I said.

"You have to fix your hair, put on some lipstick," said Mother, pushing at my limp strands of hair. "If you had worn higher heels, you would have looked better in all the dresses."

"Any higher heels and this dress would be swirling above my ankles," I snarled.

"Keeps your feet free for dancing," said the clerk.

"Allison, you are absolutely beautiful," said Mom.

I looked at her. She actually believed that. She was staring at me with her eyes all misted over with tears and a sort of trembly smile on her lips.

"I can't believe it," she said, a catch in her voice. "My little girl is all grown up."

What could I do? I told her I'd take the dress. Before I went back to the dressing room to change my clothes, I turned for one last glance in the triple mirror.

I looked about twelve years old.

12

Sunday afternoon I spent soaking in the tub, trying to soothe muscles wracked from stomping through dozens of stores, and trying to convince myself that Mom was right about the blue dress, that I was absolutely beautiful in it. My muscles felt a lot better from the hot water I kept adding to the tub, but somehow I couldn't believe the dress was anything but a horrible mistake.

About halfway through my bath, I climbed out of the tub and gave myself a facial with some sort of pink goo Mom had bought to make herself attractive for her trip. I drained the tub, filled it again, and climbed back in. I pretended the facial would do fantastic things for my face. I would be so lovely that Jerry wouldn't notice what I was wearing.

Right in the middle of my pretending, Mandy banged on the door.

"Use the downstairs bathroom!" I yelled.

"I don't have to go."

"Then beat it!" I sat up, my mood ruined. Bits of bubbles clung to my skin, but I could see most of my body was covered with wrinkles from soaking. It looked like a corpse that had been left too long for the fish to nibble on.

"Telephone!" screamed Mandy at the top of her lungs.

I yelled at her to tell them to call me back, but either she didn't hear or she ignored me, because she didn't answer. Cursing under my breath, I dragged myself out of the water, toweled off, and put on an old bathrobe.

I went into my parents' bedroom, picked up the receiver, and shoved it at my face, smearing pink goo from the facial all over it. I wiped the goo from the receiver onto my bathrobe.

"Hello!" I barked.

"Hello, Allison," said Jerry.

I lowered my voice several decibels and managed a softer tone.

"Hi, Jerry," I said.

"Hi," said Jerry. "Where have you been? I tried to call you all day yesterday, but nobody answered."

"Shopping," I said. "Trying to find a dress for the dance."

"Oh." He didn't exactly sound thrilled. "I thought maybe we might go to the movies."

"I'm sorry."

"How about tonight? It's *Casablanca,* starring Humphrey Bogart and Ingrid Bergman."

"I'd love to," I said. "Gee, that's great." My mind started racing around so I missed his next few sentences. What if Jerry came to the house? One look and he'd know my mom never could have been Miss Tennessee. He might ask to see my pet monkey. I stood, shivering and cold, and I almost cried. I could never take the chance of having Jerry come to my house, to meet my parents.

"I'll pick you up at eight," he said.

"No," I yelped. "Don't! I'll meet you at the movies."

There was a little silence. Then Jerry asked, "Why?"

" 'Cause I like to walk. As a matter of fact, I'm crazy about it."

"I'll park outside your house and we can walk from there." He sounded strained and a little bit angry.

"Fine," I said. "That's a terrific idea." I could figure something out. "I can't wait to see you," I added.

There was a cold draft around my ankles and the back of my right leg itched. I tried scratching it with the toes of my left leg, but I wasn't very successful. I bent over and was scratching with my free hand when Jerry said, "I'll come over right now and we can go for a walk."

"No!" I straightened, almost dropping the phone.

"No?"

"Er, I mean not right now." I caught a glimpse of myself in my mother's mirror over her dresser. My hair straggled in wet clumps and pink goo covered my face. The collar of my bathrobe was twisted around my neck and smeared with pink from the facial, and that was only my top half.

"You don't want me to come over?"

"I was taking a bath," I explained. "I hardly had time to dry. I'm standing here in my bathrobe."

"Oh."

"It's a long, red satin robe," I added, "but I'm still cold, because of the slit up one leg." There, that should make him think interesting thoughts about me. I grinned at the receiver.

"Well, I'd better let you go," he said.

"There's no rush." I sank down on the floor and pulled my

robe around my knees. It was warmer that way. "I like talking with you on the phone."

"In your red bathrobe."

I took a deep breath. "No," I admitted. "Actually it's my ratty old blue one."

Jerry laughed. It was the best sound I ever heard.

For a few minutes I convinced myself that everything was all right. If I only told Jerry the truth from now on and was very careful, there wouldn't be any trouble between him and me.

The first step was to prevent Jerry from meeting my parents. I told them that Jerry was tremendously shy about meeting anyone over age twenty. That worked with Dad. He went to the basement to polish golf clubs, but Mom hung around the downstairs like she always does when I have a date. I decided that it might be overeager, but that I would wait on the porch. When Jerry pulled up in his car, I would open the door, scream "Good-bye" at Mom, and then rush down the steps to meet him before he had a chance to turn off the engine.

It would have worked except that I was so horribly nervous. I kept having to run in the house to the bathroom. Even so, I almost pulled it off. I was racing for the door as Jerry crossed the porch.

"Good-bye, Mom," I yelled, grateful that at least Dad was in the basement.

"Hold on a second," said Mom.

"See you," I screamed, throwing open the door and rushing out on the porch.

Jerry had his hand raised to ring the bell. He looked very startled.

"Hello," said Mom, joining us. "You must be Jerry."

Jerry nodded, still bewildered by my fast exit. Then he

recovered. "You're Allison's mother," he said. "Miss Tennessee."

I could have died. It seemed most of the blood in my body rose to my face.

"Just a joke," I mumbled.

"More like Mrs. Glazed Doughnut," said Mom, sliding her eyes toward me. "This kid is shy?" they asked silently.

Soft and round and sweet, I thought. How could I be such an idiot? Mom didn't need to be Miss Tennessee. She was right the way she was.

"Allison says you're new here," continued Mom.

"Yes," said Jerry. "It's a lot smaller than Detroit, but I really like it." He glanced at me. "The kids are friendlier."

"That's nice." Mom smiled. "I'm glad to meet you, Jerry. Come back anytime."

"Thanks. I'd like to meet Mr. Witmer too. I guess he's off on an assignment now."

"Assignment?"

"See you, Mom," I choked, grabbing Jerry's arm and dragging him off the porch. When we were partway down the sidewalk, I turned and waved. Mom was standing on the porch, looking puzzled.

"Don't mention the spy stuff to her," I hissed at Jerry. "I shouldn't have told you that."

"Okay." He craned his neck, peering around. "I don't see any government man," he said.

"He's hiding," I explained. "He would be pretty obvious if he stood right out in the open."

"I see." He looked at me. "Are you cold or something?"

"No." I realized that I had been walking with my arms wound tightly around myself. I loosened them. "I'm a little tense," I explained.

"Any special reason?"

"My pet monkey died, the one named Alfred."

"That's too bad." Jerry reached out and took my hand, holding it in a comforting manner. Then he kept right on holding it. "Maybe you'll get another one."

"I don't think so." Jerry was holding my hand. I should have been the happiest girl on the planet, but I wasn't. I was one of the most worried ones.

Casablanca is supposed to be one of the greatest films ever made. Jerry certainly seemed to think so. Personally I don't remember very much about it. Mostly I remember sitting in the theater in a cold sweat, trying to recall everything I had told Jerry about myself and trying to figure out ways to prevent him from finding out it was all lies.

Jerry held my hand almost all through the movie and the whole way walking home. The air was damp and cool that evening, but by the time we arrived at my house, I didn't care. I was with Jerry and I was happy. I was sixteen and in love and certain that nothing was ever going to ruin it.

There was no moon that night so it was very dark out, but my front porch was brightly lit by a nearby streetlight. The light didn't seem to bother Jerry. He stood talking about school and the movie and the dance. Then he put his arms around me and leaned forward.

The curtains on our big front window sprang apart. Mandy appeared in the opening. She leaned her arms on the sill and stared out at us, her nose pushed flat against the glass.

"Is that your kid sister?" asked Jerry. He dropped his arms and stepped back.

"Yeah," I said through gritted teeth.

"The one from the movie?" He made it sound as if I had a dozen.

"Yes."

He and Amanda stared at each other from a distance of about three feet. "How old is she?"

"Five, almost six." What a perfect way to end the evening, standing on the porch, talking about Mandy.

"Shouldn't she be in bed or something?"

"Or something," I muttered, trying to make threatening gestures at Mandy without Jerry's seeing me.

"I guess I'd better go home," he said after a few awkward minutes during which I tried to decide whether to open the door and shout at Mandy or simply to pretend that she wasn't there.

"See you tomorrow!" He jumped the three steps to the walk, turned and lifted his right hand in a sort of salute, and strode to his car, whistling.

I didn't kill her. I went straight to my room and to bed, stopping only to tell Mom and Dad good-night. I stripped off my clothes and put on my nightgown and curled up in the middle of my bed. Then I rolled over on my back and stared at the white canopy. I thought of how Jerry had almost kissed me good-night. I wondered if he had, if I would have stabbed him with my pointy chin.

Then I wondered how long my luck was going to hold out. I wondered when Jerry would find out I had lied to him and when all those lies would trap me like a spider's enormous sticky web.

I wondered if Jerry would ever kiss me.

13

Thursday Jerry missed school. I first knew about it when he didn't show up for geometry class. Hans came in and slid into Jerry's seat.

"Where's Jerry?" I asked. They usually met on their way into the building in the morning.

"He didn't show up." Hans shrugged. "Maybe he missed the bus. Maybe he overslept."

Somehow I doubted it. "He could be sick," I said.

"I'll call him before lunch. Save me a seat and tell Celia why I'm late."

I nodded. Celia seemed to find more to admire about Hans every day. All week he had been eating at our table in the cafeteria. The boys who had become interested in her when she appeared as Cleopatra had finally gotten the hint and drifted to tables where girls without boyfriends were sitting.

If Jerry was really sick, he might not be well in time for the prom. I guessed I could survive if I missed the dance, and I certainly didn't mind Jerry's not seeing me dressed like a little girl, but I didn't want him to be sick. I spent the morning daydreaming about different diseases, all serious, some deadly.

My favorite daydream was the one where Jerry was very ill, and his mother called me to the house and left us alone together. Jerry was propped up in bed, his hair dark against a snowy white pillow, his face pale and strained.

I took a cool white cloth and wiped his damp forehead.

He turned his head restlessly toward me on the pillow. His velvety gray eyes opened. They were glazed with fever.

"Allison," he gasped.

I knew then that he would live. I took one of his burning hot hands in both of mine and held it to my lips.

"Jerry," I said.

In the long hours that followed I confessed my sins to him and he put a strong, gentle hand on my hair and forgave me. He knew that such insignificant past mistakes couldn't possibly stain our future happiness. We stared deeply into each other's eyes.

By the time I walked into the cafeteria at noon, I was filled with a bittersweet melancholy.

"Where's Hans?" Celia demanded.

"Making a phone call," I said. Then I sighed deeply and added, "Jerry's sick."

I had instant sympathy. Celia fussed, mostly about how horrible it would be if I missed the prom.

I sighed repeatedly and nodded, unwrapping my salami and Swiss cheese sandwich and laying out the celery sticks and Doritos Mom had packed for me. I nibbled delicately at my sandwich. Actually I was ragingly hungry, but I thought it would be unseemly to wolf down my lunch while Jerry might be on his deathbed.

Hans wasn't long. He came in and threw himself into the seat next to Celia. From his energy and the happy expression on his face, I knew his news couldn't be bad. I took a huge bite of sandwich and reached for a celery stick.

"Jerry's mother said he was up all night with a toothache," announced Hans.

I almost threw up on the table.

"A toothache isn't serious," said Hans, looking at me. "Don't worry about it. He's feeling a lot better now."

My lump of sandwich came up in my throat and went down again. I swallowed heavily and resumed breathing.

"Does it still hurt?" I asked.

"No," said Hans cheerfully. "He could have come to school, but his mother said he only fell asleep in the early morning, so she let him stay home. She was going to send him to school this afternoon, but she finally got an appointment with a dentist."

The cafeteria grew dark, then bright again. I was glad I was sitting down or I might have fallen.

"Allison, what is the matter?" asked Hans. "You turned very pale."

"Nothing," I managed. "You know the dentist's name?"

"She didn't tell me." He frowned. "It's all right. People don't die of a toothache."

Maybe Jerry won't, I thought grimly, but I could. I glanced at Celia. She knew there was something wrong all right, and it was a lot more than Jerry's aching tooth.

We skipped our bus after school and walked home. I filled Celia in on how I had told Jerry my dad was an agent for the CIA, that Dad would be sent out of town on spy assignments, and that government men watched our house while he was gone.

"There must be fifteen or twenty dentists in this town," Celia offered. "Jerry could go to any one of them."

"My dad is the only one who is softhearted enough to see a new patient on the same day they call," I said. "Besides, I'll bet half of them are already on their way to Bermuda."

"You don't know that."

I didn't answer her. I was too miserable, and she didn't push it. She walked me all the way to my house and asked if I wanted her to come in.

"No," I said. "I think I'd rather be alone today."

"Sometimes it helps when you have a bad time to share it with a friend."

"Not today."

"All right. But if you need me, call," said Celia. "I'll be home all evening."

I went into the house, put my books on the table near the foot of the stairs and put my jacket away in the closet. I hesitated. Mom was in the kitchen. Usually I go say hello to her as soon as I come home, but I was afraid I might cry and then I would have to tell her the whole thing. I didn't feel up to that.

The phone rang once, twice.

Mom answered it. I could hear her speaking in a low voice. I couldn't catch the first few words, but I heard her say, "I think she just came in. Allison! Allison, telephone!"

"I'll take it in your room," I yelled back. I walked up the stairs like a zombie, went into my parents' bedroom, and closed the door. I picked up the phone.

"Hello," I said. I could hear Mom hang up downstairs.

"This is Jerry." His voice sounded very funny, sort of blurred, probably the novocaine affecting his tongue.

"Hi," I said. "How are you?"

"Not good."

"I heard you had a bad toothache."

"It isn't my tooth."

There was a long silence. I squeezed my eyes shut against tears.

"I want to talk to you," said Jerry. "I'll come over this evening, and we'll go for one of those walks you like so much."

"Can't we talk now?" I whispered.

"No."

"I don't know if I can go out this evening."

"Make arrangements. It won't take long." He didn't even sound like Jerry, not the tone of his voice, not the stiff way he was speaking to me.

"Shouldn't you stay home and take care of yourself?" I asked. "With a new filling, and the damp air and all. I mean you don't want to take any chances."

"I don't think I have to worry about that," he said, his voice suddenly hard and clear.

"You don't?"

"No. The tooth is fine."

"I'm glad."

"I had an excellent dentist."

Here it came. I didn't say anything. I couldn't. I squeezed my eyelids tighter. I could see little rings of bright light and flashing blue stars. I couldn't shut my ears though.

"His name is Harold Witmer," said Jerry.

14

When Jerry rang the bell that evening, I was curled up on the couch in front of the big window. I had been watching the street for some time, listlessly waiting for him to arrive. I felt completely exhausted, worn out, as if I had had some bad flu and was only beginning to recover.

Mom must have known something was wrong, especially when I didn't eat any dinner, but she didn't say anything to me. She has a fine instinct about when to interfere in my life and when to keep out. Besides, she and Dad had plenty to do. They were up in their room, packing their suitcases to leave early in the morning. Mandy was watching them.

"Hello, Allison," said Jerry when I opened the door. His voice was completely flat.

"Hi. Want to come in?"

"No, thanks. Let's walk." He barely waited until I stepped out the door, then headed off the porch and down the sidewalk. I hurried to catch him, trying to match his long strides.

Jerry walked with his head down, without looking at me and most of the time without watching where he was going. He had the front of his windbreaker thrown carelessly open. His hands were jammed deep into his pants pockets.

After a few minutes, I jammed my hands into my pockets too, clenching them into fists, my fingernails pressing into my palms. I bowed my head like Jerry and walked beside him without saying a word.

We must have covered three blocks that way, like two strangers who by some coincidence are caught walking side by side, matched in pace even though they don't know each other.

"Where are we going?" I asked at last.

"The park."

The park was three more blocks. Neither one of us spoke again, not even when we passed the two-laned, brick-columned entrance of the park and descended the little hill to the tiny lake at the bottom.

In many ways it was beautiful outside, not quite dusk, the sky blue like summer. The grass was a bright lush green from the April rains, and some of the trees were beginning to leaf at last. The surface of the lake was dark and smooth, tranquil, unbroken by any movement.

It should have been a fine evening, with children playing at the edge of the water, trying to lure ducks with pieces of bread and bags of popcorn. There should have been couples walking and talking and holding hands, their laughter sharp and bright, carrying in the open air of early May.

Instead there was a nasty raw edge to the air, damp and chilling. It crept under the edges of my jacket and made me wish I had brought a scarf. My breath steamed as I took my eyes from the dark water of the lake and the lone duck that paddled on its surface to look at Jerry.

He was staring across the lake at the only other people there, a man and a small boy. The boy was trailing a stick in the water. The man was talking to him, probably trying to persuade him to throw away the stick and go someplace warm and dry.

I stamped my feet and shoved my fists deeper into the pockets of my jacket.

Jerry looked at me. His eyes said that he didn't know me and more, that he didn't think he ever wanted to know me.

"Why did you tell me your father was a spy?"

I opened my mouth, closed it again.

"Why, Allison? Why would you tell me such a thing?" His voice was loud, too loud. I was glad the man and the boy were leaving. No one else was near the lake to hear Jerry yell at me.

"I don't know," I said.

"But you must! I believed you!"

"I didn't mean to—"

"Sure," he said bitterly. "You thought up this wild story to tell me and I was dumb enough to believe it."

"I'm sorry," I managed.

"You're sorry! Is that all you can say?"

He was staring at me, hard. I risked a glance at him, then looked across the lake. I wanted to run all the way home, up to my room and throw myself on my bed under the white canopy, to bury myself under my blankets and hide forever, while life outside went on without me and everyone forgot there ever was an Allison Witmer.

"I wanted you to notice me," I said, "so I tried to make everything about myself more interesting."

96

"What was so bad about the truth?"

"Then you only thought of me as a buddy," I said. "Anyone can have a father who's a dentist."

"Your father seems like a great guy," said Jerry. "Isn't he good enough for you?"

Not good enough? I thought of my father and I felt awful. I thought of my mother and I said, "My mother isn't Miss Tennessee. She never was. I made that up too, and I'm sorry. They are good enough for me. Too good. It's just—"

"That you didn't think they were good enough for me!" He grabbed me by one arm. "What kind of a jerk do you think I am?"

"Jerry—"

He took a deep breath. Then he noticed his hand was holding my arm and dropped it. He cleared his throat.

It was growing dark, but Jerry's face stood out white against the trees. He walked toward one, turned around and looked at me again. He shoved his hands back into his pockets; his shoulders slumped. His voice was softer. I had to come close to hear him.

"What other lies did you tell me?" he asked.

I bit my lower lip. My stomach lurched and I was glad I hadn't eaten any dinner. I stared at the ground, shivered, and said, "I don't have a pet monkey; I never did. I wasn't ever bitten by a rabid dog, and I don't know a thing about tennis." I paused. "That wasn't true about Stephanie either. She never did drugs; she was never picked up by the police."

"I didn't believe that. You said it was only a rumor."

"A rumor I started."

"Oh, Allison." He sounded absolutely sick.

"I'm sorry."

"And that's supposed to make everything all right?"

"No." I shook my head, overcome by enormous sorrow. "Jerry, I tell lies. I always have. I try, and most of the time —the last year or two anyway—I manage not to. I thought I was cured. I really did. But then I met you, and I liked you so much, and I—I—"

"What?"

"I never thought you could be interested in me, so I started making these things up, and then I couldn't stop."

Jerry leaned against the tree. He looked very tired, but he didn't look angry anymore, only very sad. "You know a funny thing?" he said.

I waited.

"I liked you a lot."

"And now?"

"I don't know. I thought you were better than that."

I *am* better than that! I wanted to scream, but of course I didn't. I didn't say anything.

It was quite dark now. I could barely see Jerry's face. After a few minutes he shrugged away from the tree and said, "Come on. It's cold here. I'd better walk you home."

I followed him out of the park. An ugly thing happened, and I hoped it was over. Somehow I couldn't ever imagine telling anyone about it, not Celia, not my mom, not anybody.

We walked side by side in the dark toward my house. When we came to the streetlight out front, I stopped. Jerry took two more steps and stopped also, turning, his face reflecting the cold blue from the light.

"I'll understand if you don't want to take me to the dance," I said.

"I'll take you to the dance."

"You don't have to."

"I know." His mouth twisted. He glanced at the house, eager to be away from me. The curtains covering the front window fell straight and smooth. No Mandy pushed them aside that evening.

"Good night," he said abruptly.

As he walked around his car to the driver's door, he struck one clenched fist viciously against a fender.

15

I made it through all of Friday, saying good-bye to my parents in the morning, through school and through the long
evening alone with Mandy, by faking it. It wasn't difficult.
Since my parents left early for the plane, Jerry ignored me
completely at school, and all Mandy wanted to do was eat
junk food and watch television, it was really quite simple.

I planned to get through most of Saturday by sleeping as
long as possible. I made a pretty good effort. It was after ten
when Mandy woke me by tugging at the hem of my nightgown.

"Someone wants you on the phone," she said. She was still
in her pajamas. Her face needed to be washed and she car-
ried a bowl of Cap'n Crunch in one hand, stuffing the cereal
into her mouth with the other.

"Okay," I muttered, raising myself on my elbows, then climbing out of bed. "Go get dressed, will you."

"I'm watching cartoons."

"Get dressed and then watch cartoons." I stumbled around, pulling on my bathrobe, rubbing at my eyes. My mouth was very dry; my tongue felt large and furry.

"Hello," I said, picking up the receiver.

"This is Barry O'Neill, Ron's roommate."

Ron's roommate. My heart leapt, then settled slowly and painfully in my chest. This had to be bad news and I didn't want to hear it.

"Yes," I said.

"Ron's sick."

"Oh, no."

"He has food poisoning."

I must have said something, but I don't know what.

"Most of the kids in our dorm spent the whole night throwing up," said Barry, sounding very cheerful about the whole thing. "The school nurses made a sickroom down in the cafeteria. The rest of us have to go to Miller Hall to eat."

"How is Ron?"

"He'll be okay. They didn't have to take anyone to the hospital."

"Then he can't come home." The truth was beginning to dawn.

"No, he can't," said Barry. "Not only is he sick, but the guy he was riding with is too. Ron feels really bad about it."

"That's okay," I said, trying not to cry. "You're sure he'll be all right?"

"Yeah. He said he'd call you tomorrow."

Somehow I got off the line and sat on the floor, feeling like a lump of wet clay. No Ron meant no one to watch Mandy. And no one to watch Mandy meant no dance. I didn't know whether to be sorry or relieved. I sat there for a few minutes trying to decide, then got up and headed to my room to get dressed.

Mandy was still there, standing near my dresser. She had a guilty expression in her faded blue eyes.

"That was Ron's roommate," I said. "Ron can't come home. He's sick."

She took it in and then asked, "Who's going to watch me?"

"I am."

"I can watch myself."

"You can not. You're only a little kid." I went over to my dresser to see what she had been messing in. Mandy edged toward the door.

Just as I'd suspected, it was the Spunsugar nail polish I had borrowed from Celia. Mandy hadn't put the cap on right. I loosened it, then tightened it correctly. Then I glanced at my Shirley Temple doll.

Her faded lips were a bright shiny pink. I leaned forward, horrified. Her nails were painted, and the tiny roses in her nosegay were a soggy lacquered pink.

"What did you do?" I screamed.

"I made her pretty again." Mandy sounded small and scared.

"You ruined her! I told you a million times to keep out of my room! You're always wrecking things!" Suddenly the last two days were just too much for me. I sat on the side of my bed, covered my face with my hands, and cried.

When I finally finished sobbing and blowing my nose, I felt a little bit better. I dressed in some jeans and an old shirt and went downstairs. The door to Mandy's room was closed. When I went past it, I thought of telling her I forgave her, but I decided to wait. That kid had messed in my stuff once too often.

I must have made twenty phone calls that morning, trying to find a sitter. Of course I couldn't locate a single one. They all were either going to the dance or had been called weeks ago by parents eager to attend the Elks' ball or to go to the Country Club.

Finally, in desperation, I called Mrs. Owens. Perhaps she had a spare sitter on her list. I doubted it from the way she had been after me for that night, but I was willing to try anything.

"Allison," she said. "You can watch the boys?"

"No," I told her. "I called to find out if you know anyone who's free this evening. My brother Ron is sick and can't come home to watch Mandy. If I can't find a sitter, I can't go to the prom." My voice was shaky from emotion and hoarse from all my talking on the phone.

"Oh," she said. "Well, we don't have a sitter either." There was a silence during which we both breathed heavily. Then she said, "But I do have an idea."

I held my breath.

"Why don't you bring Amanda over here? She can play with John and Jeremy and Jason."

That certainly was nice of Mrs. Owens.

"It won't be a bit more trouble for you to watch four instead of three."

"I don't think I can," I said.

"If you aren't going to the dance—" Mrs. Owens is all heart.

"I'm not sure of that yet." My tones were icy but I really didn't care. At that moment I determined I was going to do anything, even watch television that evening, rather than baby-sit the Owens' kids.

"If you change your mind, call me," she said.

I didn't slam down the receiver. I lowered it slowly, looking at the kitchen clock. It was time for lunch. I took a deep, trembling breath and decided I had better call Jerry before I prepared the tuna fish salad and called Mandy to the table.

Jerry wasn't happy to hear from me. He was even less happy when he heard I was calling to cancel our date.

"Listen," he said. "I rented a tux. I bought a corsage. The least you can do is put on your dress and go."

"But I can't go," I said. "I already told you. My parents are away and my brother Ron has food poisoning at college."

"Where are your parents?" he asked, suspicion darkening his voice.

"In Bermuda."

"Sure."

"Jerry, they really are in Bermuda and my brother really is sick."

"Tell me about it."

"I have enough trouble," I said. "I know I lied to you and you don't trust me anymore, but this time I am telling the truth."

"I don't believe you."

"Okay," I said, and hung up.

While I made the tuna salad, I told myself that actually the prom was a very trivial event in a lifetime of huge important affairs and that I was surprised I could be bothered to go to it in the first place. I told myself that my love for Jerry was only an adolescent crush and I should be grateful for the miserable experience I had, because at least I had learned never to lie again. I told myself all that and a lot more, but I wasn't one bit happier when I was finished.

I put the salad on the plates on the kitchen table. Then I put out bread and glasses of milk. I went to the bottom of the stairs and yelled up for Mandy. She didn't answer.

She was probably back in my room messing around again,

or else she was sulking and refused to answer. I went upstairs after her.

She wasn't in my room. I inspected the Shirley Temple doll to see if I could clean it but it was hopeless. The nail polish had soaked through the little nosegay onto the gown. I put the doll back on my dresser.

I paused at the doorway of my room to look at my bulletin board. I looked first of the picture of Jerry, my most recent acquisition, and then at the coloring of the evil man with a sack of candy that Mandy had given me. Shaking my head, I went to her room. I tapped on the door and then opened it.

She wasn't there.

The curtains in the room were still drawn from the night. I went across and opened them, looking around the room as I did so. It was painted all white, with a dark green rug and green curtains. Mandy's bed was unmade, the ruffled bedspread dragging on the rug, a pile of comic books in the nest she had made from the blankets. More comics were scattered on the floor.

On her desk there was a stack of books from the library, one of my teen magazines, and the tube of lipstick I had given her. Her pajamas were draped over a chair. Beside the chair on the floor was a half-empty bowl of Cap'n Crunch.

It was at that moment I felt the first small, cold, uneasy fear in me.

"Mandy?" I said. Then I shouted, "Mandy! Lunchtime!"

The house was completely silent. The hair on the back of my neck rose.

"I'm not mad anymore," I shouted. "You can come out now. It's time to eat."

There was a quality of silence that made me certain I was alone. I searched the house anyway, under the beds, in the closets, in the basement. I even looked behind the furnace into the dark spidery hole that used to be a place to store coal.

The tuna salad was limp on the plates in the kitchen. I wasn't hungry. I covered the plates with plastic wrap and shoved them into the refrigerator. My hands were cold and there was a dull ache in my stomach.

I went to the back door.

"Mandy," I called.

Our yard looked very small and empty. When I called the second time, a robin flew up from the rosebush near the garage and onto the maple tree nearby. There was no other movement. The clear outside air sounded as empty as the house.

16

It was one of the most beautiful spring days I have ever seen. The sky was a deep, intense blue that seemed to go on forever, with only an occasional fluffy white cloud drifting lazily across it. The air was clear and quiet, filled with the scent of new grass and flowers, and the temperature was perfect, not hot and not cold.

It was a good day for anything except trying to find my little sister who had been driven away by my screams of rage and probably lay crushed under the wheels of a car. Or maybe even worse, she could have been captured by some pervert with a sack of candy behind his back.

Mandy wouldn't go with a stranger, I tried to tell myself as I stomped around the block, calling her name, going into yards and checking bushes. She's a smart little kid; she wouldn't fall for the old sack-of-candy trick.

"Mandy!" I called for the thousandth time. By now everyone within blocks must have known she had run away or was lost. I had knocked on loads of doors, asking for her. Everyone else could hear me shouting.

I had kept the Morgans' woods to search last, perhaps because I suspected that if she were hiding, that was where she would go. If I didn't find her in the woods, I didn't think I could face life.

I hesitated on the edge between the back of our lot and the woods. I hated that dark, damp place; I don't really know why. Mandy liked it well enough. I looked at the ground, knocked over a mushroom with one sneaker and flattened it beneath my foot. Then I set about methodically covering the woods.

I checked the tree house first. I didn't expect to find her there because of what I had told her about turning into a toad, but I checked it anyway. Then I swear I beat through every bush in the entire lot. If someone had seen me, they would have thought I was searching for a small cat or a guinea pig instead of a five-year-old girl.

My mood was not improved by returning to the house and finding it empty.

I didn't know what to do. One minute I was sick with worry over what had happened to Mandy, what some monster could be doing to her right this very instant, and the next minute I was consumed by rage, planning different kinds of ugly punishment for when the little brat did turn up. I paced nervously about the downstairs of the house, stopping to stare out windows, at the phone, willing it to ring, for someone to say Mandy was with them and all right. Twice I actually lifted it to call the police, then put it down in a spasm of indecision.

The doorbell rang, cutting through the hideous silence of the house and making me jump. I ran to answer it.

Jerry was standing on the porch.

"Jerry!" I screamed, throwing myself at him. I hung on to him as hard as I could. Then I burst into tears.

Jerry held me for a couple of seconds, then untangled himself and stepped back a foot to look at me.

I was howling and bawling like a little kid, but I couldn't force myself to stop.

"I knew the prom was important to girls," said Jerry, "but I never knew it was this important."

"Forget the stupid dance," I said through my tears. "I don't care about the dance." I told him the whole story, pausing in the middle for a trip to the kitchen for a wad of tissues to mop my eyes and blow my nose. Jerry followed and dropped into a seat opposite me at the table.

Finally I got some control of myself and subsided into sniveling and wishing I were dead.

"Why did you come?" I asked. "To check on me, make sure I wasn't lying again?"

"I wanted to talk to you," said Jerry. "I didn't like that phone call."

"Well, neither did I."

"It seems all of a sudden everything between us is all messed up."

"And I suppose that is all my fault?"

"Hey. It sure isn't mine." His gray eyes were hard as marbles, nothing soft or warm about them.

"I don't want to fight," I said. "I don't even have time to fight." I glanced at the clock over the stove, wondering exactly how long Mandy had been gone. "I have enough trouble right now."

"Actually I came over to make up," said Jerry.

"You did?" I laughed, the sound hopeless—the way I felt. "How do you know I won't say 'okay' and be lying again?"

"I don't."

He looked so bleak that I wanted to touch him and tell him not to worry, but I didn't. Instead I promised to prove to Jerry I would never deceive him again, to bite off my treacherous tongue if it ever so much as threatened to lie.

"We'll work it out," I said. "I have a heart of gold."

"I know." He grinned.

"My heart of gold would feel a lot better right now if I could find Mandy," I said. "I'm getting scared." With a great effort, I managed not to start crying again.

"I sure hope my parents are having a good time," I added, "because when they get home they're going to find my brother dead of food poisoning, my sister in the hands of some pervert, and me in the hospital with a nervous breakdown."

"Come on now," said Jerry. "Your brother will be all right and your little sister is only hiding out somewhere."

"What would you know about it?" I sniffed.

"Believe me, I know about little sisters," said Jerry.

"Yeah?" I eyed him suspiciously.

"I have three of them."

"Three!"

"Yep, and a younger brother."

"You never told me that!"

He shrugged. "You never asked."

I dabbed at my nose with a tissue, wondering if it were red, and if my eyes were a blaze of pink. I have never been an attractive crier.

"Mandy could have stayed at my house tonight. With all those kids no one would have noticed," he said, "but two of my sisters have strep and my brother has the chicken pox. My mother is going nutty trying to keep them apart."

"Thanks anyway," I said listlessly.

"Tell you what—" Jerry looked at me. "Did you have lunch?"

"No." I sighed. "That's when I discovered Mandy was gone. I made some tuna salad and called her. I shoved it in the fridge when she didn't come."

Jerry opened the refrigerator. He took out one of the plates of salad and a glass of milk.

"You are going to eat this, and then we are going to go looking for her together," he said.

"I couldn't eat a thing."

"You are going to." He put the plate in front of me, shoved a fork at me, and commanded, "Eat!"

I wondered vaguely whether Jerry were a male chauvinist pig under his fine exterior, or if he were merely masterful. Then I dug into the tuna salad.

All of a sudden I was starved. I wolfed down the salad, drank my milk, and ate two pieces of bread. Jerry watched as if he thought my behavior were full of grace and style.

"I hate to see women pick at their food," he said. "I took Stephanie over to Arby's one evening, and all she had was a small Coke and two of my french fries."

It was all right with me if he liked women who gorged themselves, but I thought it was a little unfeeling of him to bring up Stephanie Harris under the circumstances.

"Now let's look for your sister," he said.

"Do you want the other plate of tuna salad?" I asked, remembering my manners.

"She'll want it," he said. "She must be hungry by now. Let's check out the woods you mentioned."

"I already searched every inch," I said. "There couldn't be a rabbit hiding in there."

"Yeah, but I bet you called and made a lot of noise while you looked and she's hiding from you. I think we ought to sneak up on her. Let's try that tree house first."

"I looked there," I said. "Besides, she would never go back there, because I told her—" I caught myself.

"Told her what?"

"That if she played in there, she would turn into a toad," I blurted, my cheeks burning.

Jerry laughed.

"Come on," he said. He grabbed one of my hands. "We'll find her."

If I hadn't been so worried, I would have felt like a fool, creeping through the Morgans' woods with Jerry. We crouched low, silently pushing through bushes and skirting trees. I felt a little bit as if I were back seven or eight years ago, playing cowboys and Indians with Ron.

"There's the tree house," I whispered.

"That thing?" It's barely off the ground."

"The Morgans didn't want their kids to fall out of it and break something."

He eyed the little room of weathered wood. "Wait until I go around to the other side. That way she can't escape without our catching her."

He did believe Mandy was hiding there. I felt a surge of optimism, despite the fact I had checked the tree house only an hour before.

Jerry left, making a big arc around the small structure. I stayed where I was, waiting until he situated himself on the far side and waved me forward.

I approached as quietly as I could, leaned around the nearest solid side of the house and peered into the opening.

Mandy was sitting on the floor, curled in a little ball, her arms wrapped around the muddy knees of her jeans. She looked as if she were asleep, but at the squeal I made when I spotted her, her eyes flew open.

"Mandy!" I yelled. "What are you doing here?"

"Hiding."

I crawled into the tree house beside her and grabbed her in my arms, anxious to reassure myself that she was there, that she hadn't been snatched by some pervert with a sack of candy.

"Let me go!" She wiggled.

"In a minute." I hugged her tighter, aware that Jerry was coming to the opening of the tree house. "I can't believe I've found you. I've been looking for you for hours!"

"You have?" She sounded skeptical.

"I almost called the police," I said, my relief mixing with anger. "Why did you run away?"

"So you could go to the dance. Then you wouldn't be mad at me anymore."

"Weren't you scared?"

"Of what?"

"You know. Of men with sacks of candy."

"That's just something you and Mom and a bunch of teachers made up," she said scornfully.

My mouth went dry. "The stories about tooth fairies and toads and stuff like that are made up," I said. "The stories about strangers who steal little kids and do horrible things to them are not. There are some very bad people in the world." Relishing the feel of her wiry little body, I buried my nose in her soft fuzzy hair.

"Uck," I said, drawing back in a hurry. I wish I could say that she was all sweet and little and fragrant, but that kid smelled exactly like an elementary school classroom, one that hadn't been aired all winter.

"You stink!" I said.

"Yeah," said Mandy, a certain amount of pleasure in her voice.

"When was the last time you had a bath?"

"Wednesday," she said proudly.

"Well, you are going to have another one as soon as you eat lunch. You smell awful."

She was completely unmoved by my assessment of her

physical charms. "Is that Prince Charming?" she asked, staring at Jerry.

Jerry grinned.

"That's Jerry Hamilton," I said. I could feel my ears growing very hot. I hoped my hair covered them. "You remember. He was at the Charlie Chaplin movie."

"Oh, yeah," she said. Her faded blue eyes looked canny as she assessed Jerry.

"If you let me pet your horse," she said, "I'll give you the money I've been saving."

"Horse?"

"The white—"

"Mandy, go back to the house," I ordered.

"But—"

"Now!" I was almost sorry we had found her.

"But I want to pet his big white charger," she whined.

"Mandy—" I could have strangled her. Instead, I bit the inside of my cheek and stared steadily, challengingly, at Jerry.

He didn't laugh. He looked gravely at Mandy and said, "I'm sorry but my white charger has gone back to his stables in Siberia and won't be available until you're thirteen."

"You're joking me," accused Mandy, tilting her head to one side.

"You are absolutely right."

"You never even had a white charger."

"Right again." He leaned forward, putting his hands on the floor of the tree house and staring at her. "I'll tell you what I do have, which is a lot scarier than a big white charger."

"What?"

"Three little sisters."

"Oh, sure."

"*And* a little brother."

114

"You're lying," said Mandy.

"Cross my heart."

She looked slightly less suspicious.

"If you behave yourself and don't give Allison any more trouble," he continued, "she and I will take you and them, the whole herd, on a picnic in the park the day after school is out."

"Whoopee!" she shrieked, tumbling out of the tree house.

"Go on back to the house and wash your hands," I instructed. "I'll be right there to get your lunch."

Mandy ran off toward the house, waggling her arms like an airplane, dodging trees and bushes.

Jerry and I stood alone for a moment in the little clearing in the grove of trees. Then we walked slowly after her. Neither of us said anything until we came to the four steps to my back door. Jerry stopped there.

"I'm sorry we can't go to the dance," he said. "I know you would have been beautiful, and we would have had a great time."

I nodded, not trusting my voice. The prom, even the prom in my little-girl dress, seemed like an impossibly beautiful dream.

"Tell you what," he said when I didn't answer. "How would you like to go to the movies and then over to Max's Place afterward?"

"What about Mandy?"

"We'll take her with us."

"On our date?"

"Why not?" He leaned on the rusty wrought-iron banister leading up the steps to my back door. "We can go to other dances. Tonight we can take your little sister to see Fred Astaire and Rita Hayworth in *You'll Never Get Rich*." His velvety eyes looked into mine.

"Okay," I said. I'm afraid I didn't sound very enthusiastic.

"I'll come by early, about seven. I can leave the car here and we can walk to the movies and then to Max's Place." He smiled at me. "We'll have a good time. You wait and see."

"I know we will." This time I managed to sound as if I believed it.

"That's my girl," said Jerry. He touched me gently with one finger under my pointy chin. "I'll see you at seven."

Jerry left the back way, and I climbed the four steps and went into the house. "That's my girl" kept repeating in my brain. Not "my buddy" but "my girl."

17

So that is how I came to go to an old movie and to Max's Place afterward while everyone else went to the prom. I know that day should be remembered by me forever as The Great Dance Disaster, but from the moment Jerry called me "my girl," my spirits started rising.

It was almost as if so many things had gone wrong that things had to start to go right. I pinned the corsage of tiny yellow roses Jerry had bought me on the white embroidered top Mom had picked out at the Speciality Sports Shoppe. I have never looked better, not even as Tokyo Rose. I have never been happier either.

Mandy was no trouble at all. As a matter of fact, she hardly seemed to be with us, at least until the three of us came up the walk to our porch shortly before midnight. At that point, I began to wonder how I was going to get rid of her for a few minutes. I could hardly say, "Amanda, go on in the house. I want to kiss Jerry good-night."

I looked at her.

Jerry looked at her.

Mandy looked back.

"Why don't you run along inside now and get ready for bed," I suggested pleasantly.

"No."

"Mandy, go on."

She looked at the porch floor and dug with the toe of one shoe.

"Jerry," I said. "You're the expert with little sisters. You handle this."

Jerry cleared his throat. Then he said, "Sometimes you can go places with your sister and me and other times you can't. But you are going to be a lot more welcome if you let us alone when we ask. Understand?"

"Yeah."

"Then go in the house now. Allison and I want to be alone."

"Why?"

"Just go!"

"Okay." She paused after she had the door open. "Good night, Prince Charming," she said.

"Good night," said Jerry. "And don't look out the window!"

The door closed softly and Amanda was gone. She didn't look out the window either. I resisted the urge to duck my head and dig at the porch floor with the toe of one shoe the way she had. Instead, I stared up at Jerry. He stared down at me. His face came slowly closer to mine.

At that moment the pin holding my corsage gave way, and the whole thing fell off.

I knelt to pick it up and Jerry knelt too. I held the little bouquet of yellow flowers in my hands and glanced at him. His lips touched mine. His kiss was even better than I dreamed it would be.

When we stood, he kissed me again. At that moment I knew that the night Jerry and I went with my little sister to an old movie instead of the prom was going to be remembered by me as one of the very best evenings of my whole entire life.

And that's the truth.

About the Author

"Because this book is a teenage romance," says author Nancy J. Hopper, "the moving factor behind the plot is the boy-girl relationship. However, my main interest was in working with a character who had everything going for her —intelligence, appearance, and personality—but who had one overwhelming defect. Allison told lies: not just little lies, but huge structures of deceit. The involvement and suspense in writing came not so much from the question of could Allison get Jerry, but could she keep him if she got him, and just how long could she continue before her entire construction of lies came crashing down on her."

Nancy J. Hopper's novels for young people include *Secrets*; *The Seven½ Sins of Stacey Kendall*; *Just Vernon*; and *Hang On, Harvey!* She lives in Alliance, Ohio.